Pestilence
Susie Kearley

Chapter 1
The Ethical Dilemma

"This drug is our greatest achievement to date!" said Dr Leeman, research scientist. "It kills everything - MRSA, drug-resistant tuberculosis, different strains of influenza, it might even help eradicate the common cold!"

He did a high-five with his colleagues, grinning from ear to ear and waved the papers in the air. "This is going to transform medicine, and put the company on the map. We can grow, expand, do more good in the world. I'm so blimmin' excited!"

As they started to plan clinical trials, people with untreatable conditions were put forward by their clinicians, hoping for a cure, and among those selected to take part was Terry White, who'd be testing a topical application, designed for difficult-to-treat skin complaints.

* * *

"This is a great opportunity," Terry explained nervously, as she broached the subject with her partner, Alex. "They think it could help me."

"I don't care. There's no way you're taking part in clinical trials for a new drug."

"But..."

"But nothing! They torture innocent animals for pure commercial gain! You know that!"

"I'm desperate!" Terry pleaded. "The animal testing stage is over now. Me taking part won't change what's happened. I'm volunteering to *be* the lab rat. I'm taking the risk."

"No you're not."

"Oh please Alex - try to understand. My contribution might mean the drug eventually helps people - and it might help me! I'm in so much pain!"

"No way!" he scowled. "You're a hypocrite. Where's your conscience? I can't believe you want to be a part of that!" His face reddened - hints of madness in his eyes. "I spent a year in jail for standing up to those barbarians! If you do this, we're finished," he declared unequivocally. "This is the ugliest form of capitalism. Totally sick."

Tears welled up in Terry's eyes. "I've been so ill, for so long..." her voice trailed off, choked with emotion, "You haven't been here to see all the pain."

"No! I've been in jail for standing up to legalised murder. Then when I come out you're ready to support the torture and murder of innocent animals for your own selfish gain? You're no better than the vivisectionists themselves!"

She was broken. He turned angrily, to leave in disgust. He paused by the door, "All those years we spent protesting against animal testing. You're a total charlatan - protesting with me all those years, and then turning around and joining them!" He slammed the door on his way out.

She choked back the tears and telephoned her old friend and former nurse, Sheila.

"Hey, nice to hear from you," said Sheila. "How you doing? Still excited about the trials?"

"It's all gone wrong," said Terry.

"How so?"

"Alex is furious about my plans to take part. I feel numb."

"But you've been in pain for years."

"Exactly."

"He should be behind you on this."

"I thought that too, but he isn't."

"That's not on. Not supportive at all."

"I feel really awful going against him, but these unexplained sores..." she fidgeted. "I can't get comfortable. I can't live a normal life! This is a chance of normality! A stab at happiness! I can't let the opportunity pass me by."

"No. And I don't think you should. If Alex really loved you, he'd want you to get well. Boycotting something that could make you well isn't going to put an end to the life-sciences industry."

"That's how I feel. It wasn't a decision I took lightly. We've tried protesting and lobbying, to end the animal testing - demanding they find alternative ways of testing things. We've failed, but I've

4

never objected to human 'guinea pigs' - now I want to be one. This opportunity could change my life."

"Stick with it girl. You don't need him. Do what's right for you."

"Thank you," said Terry.

"You're welcome. Stay in touch."

Terry hung up, conflicted. Sad, but thoughtful. Still quietly optimistic.

She thought fondly of the time she first met Alex, protesting against animal testing and vivisection in a demonstration outside Huntingdon Life Sciences 20 years earlier. *We were both so passionate. No wonder he ended up in jail - he always took things too far and wouldn't let this go! One of the reasons I fell for him.* She smiled to herself. *Rebel.*

Alex had served time for his involvement in a campaign of terror against employees of Huntingdon Life Sciences, first when they were just teenagers, and then more recently against a research facility at Oxford University.

I understand his passion, but after years of physical pain, this is a life-changing opportunity.... I just want to take part, she thought.

*   *   *

Alex sat in the pub, feeling utterly betrayed, angry, and bitterly disappointed. "I can't believe she'd do this!" he said to the barman as he tried to drown his sorrows. "We were a team. We stood up to those imbeciles together. How can someone so committed to ending animal testing just turn around and take part in human trials?"

"She's putting herself at risk - not the animals - so she might see it differently," suggested the barman.

"But she's supporting the industry - it can't go to market without human trials, so she's just an integral part of the process." He sipped his drink. "It's unforgivable. I loved that girl. I thought she was my soul mate. But I don't see how we can get past this... unless she comes to her senses."

"Has she been in a lot of pain?" asked the barman.

"Yes," Alex admitted. "The past year, while I've been away, has been awful for her." He stared into his drink. "I thought she was managing her condition quite well before that, but perhaps the stress of being on her own was too much."

5

"It sounds like she's had a lot to deal with."

"She has," conceded Alex. "We've tried all sorts of things. Nutritional approaches and herbal remedies, even drugs - against my better judgement. She had a bad reaction to them!"

"Perhaps she thinks it's her last chance?"

"Bullshit. There are always new things you can try without resorting to this."

"That's probably true."

They stood in silence as Alex shuffled on his bar stool and kicked against the wooden veneer - restless, uncomfortable, irritated, annoyed, overwhelmed by feelings of betrayal. Yet also, quietly feeling like perhaps he'd let Terry down by his absence, by his failure to find a natural cure. Perhaps it was partly his fault.

"Look... I do understand her dilemma," he confessed quietly. "I've been there some of the time - every time I got out of the slammer, trying to soothe her pain with natural remedies and special diets. Sometimes they helped for a while, but often they had little lasting benefit. I do sympathise..."

He sipped his drink and then slammed it down on the bar, spilling it on the bar mat. "But after everything we've been through together, how can she turn her back on everything we believe in? Everything we've fought for!"

The barman shrugged, "I feel your pain mate. It's hard."

When Alex returned home that night, he slept in the spare room.

Chapter 2
The Breakthrough

BBC Television News: "Scientists have announced a medical breakthrough that could see disease-causing bacteria and viruses eradicated with one powerful pill or topical potion. The new drug has been developed from a previously unknown species of jelly fungus that's become prolific across the UK. Known as Kaylmycotopa - Kayl for short - it thrives in our warming climate, so is easy to grow, and it has medicinal qualities like nothing we've ever seen before."

The camera zoomed in on an example of Kayl. "Its antibacterial qualities were discovered accidentally by a microbiology student at University College London who took an interest in the new species, and since then, there's been interest in its medicinal potential from scientists around the world. Now extracts are being studied. Dr David Leeman from Cother Pharmaceuticals explains..."

Dr Leeman: "It's very exciting. This drug appears to have unparalleled antibacterial properties, so we're expecting to make big advances in the fight against antibiotic-resistant bacteria. There's more work to do to understand the drug's full potential - it has antiviral qualities too and the research is extremely promising."

"What's made the fungi show up now?" asked the reporter. "We're seeing it turn up in our parks and gardens. It's quite invasive."

"It appears to be an evolutionary adaptation as a result of global warming," the scientist explained. "The warm humid atmosphere provides the perfect environment for fungi to mutate and thrive. This is a highly adaptable species, which has successfully proliferated across the British countryside and is now finding its way into our towns too. It's thought to be a mutation of a much older but less invasive type of jelly fungus. The great news is that extracts of Kayl appear to hold the answer to antibiotic resistance, and it has a whole load of other potential uses too."

"That sounds exciting," said the reporter, "but some people are eating it raw, claiming it gives them an emotional lift and makes them feel better. Is that safe?"

Leeman frowned, "We don't know the full effects of consuming it raw, so I wouldn't recommend consumption. It could be dangerous. The compounds we're working with are extracts - the beneficial elements - which we'll develop to their optimal potential. Any adverse effects are monitored and the end product will be designed so that side-effects are kept to a minimum. Like some other species of fungi, Kayl can cause severe gastrointestinal problems, hallucinations, and it can lead to paranoia and serious mental health problems. People shouldn't self-medicate."

"That sounds like good advice Dr Leeman, so can you tell us more about its potential medicinal uses?"

"I can't say too much because there's a bit of a race to be the first to bring the medicine safely to market, but we will be doing human trials to ascertain safety, efficacy, and its potential use in a wide variety of medical applications."

Chapter 3
A Solid Investment

"Have you got a progress report for us David?" asked Robert, the company director at Cother Pharmaceuticals, "It was good to see you representing us on the news. The interview went well."

"Yes," he replied, "It feels surreal being on TV! Just glad my mind didn't go blank!"

"Come and see some potential investors - they're in my office and want to know more about the potential of Kayl."

"OK. Let me grab a coffee and I'll be with you!" Leeman went to the drinks machine, opted for an expresso to keep his mind sharp, and returned to see the investors in the director's office with papers in his hand. They were smart, young, and hungry for good opportunities.

"This promises to be one of the most remarkable breakthroughs in medical history," he explained, "possibly more significant than the discovery of penicillin."

There was an air of excitement and the men were keen to know more. "The fungal extracts are incredibly powerful," continued Leeman. "As an antibiotic, the new drug has the potential to wipe out MRSA. As an anti-viral, it could become a tool against the common cold or even HIV. There's no time to waste because our competitors are aware of its potential too, and we need to be the first to market with a patented product. The opportunity to capitalise on this is huge." He handed out forecasts.

"There's no shortage of the raw ingredient, which should make mass production relatively cheap and easy. The fungus is thriving in the wild. It's prolific, even invasive, so it should be easy to farm quickly to meet our needs."

Some of the businessmen nodded knowingly. "I've experienced the fungi's invasion first hand!" said one.

"Me too! Can't get rid of the blasted stuff!" said another. "It's resistant to fungicide, weed killer, even bleach! It seems to me that the only way to remove the jelly from the ground is to scrape it up and throw it away!"

There was a jovial laugh around the table, as they all empathised.

"I add it to my compost heap," said another investor.

"I heap it into the dustbin!" said the first. "It's everywhere! Turning up on the edge of lawns and playgrounds, under the hedgerows. My kids gather it up and throw it at each other, like flaky snowballs!" It was a jovial exchange, generating a lot of interest in the investment opportunity.

As the meeting came to an end, the businessmen talked among themselves. There was an air of excitement about the new development, with many nods, smiles, and positive remarks. During the driest summers, the fungus dehydrated and shrunk into the ground, but it always returned as soon as the damp set in and the humidity rose.

*   *   *

The following day Leeman discussed the project with his bright young lab assistant, Pete Ward. "People underestimate the power of different fungi. They're a remarkable species, with the power to heal or to kill. People don't treat fungi with the respect they deserve."

The lad nodded amiably. He perhaps underestimated fungi too, as he didn't really know what Leeman was talking about. *To heal or to kill?* He understood its healing potential; after all, penicillin was developed from a mould. But death by fungi – that's pretty unusual isn't it?

As if reading his thoughts, Leeman added, "Fungal infections are a real threat to people's recovery in oncology, you know. Once you've been treated for cancer with radiation and chemo, your immune system's so trashed that fungal infections can get a grip and kill you - when your immune system's down and you have little defence."

"Oh. Nasty." replied Ward. He was just out of college and still in training. He pulled a disgusted face. "Sounds gross."

"Well there's a lot going on in the development of antifungals too, so the outlook's not too bad, but you need to treat these microbes with respect. There are new treatments available now to harness the power of the immune system with

10

immunotherapy, so the future's much brighter for people with difficult-to-treat infections, than it was in the past."

"But we still don't have a cure for MRSA, or anything to treat the common cold!" said Ward.

"That's where these new drugs come in," said Leeman. "Our latest research with mice shows that Kayl extracts have remarkable potential in both those areas. It might eventually lead to a treatment for some virulent strains of flu, but viruses are so prone to adaptation and mutation, it's hard to imagine finding an effective and universal cure for all cold viruses."

"It's great progress though. I've got some catching up to do!"

"You'll get there," Leeman reassured him. "We're starting to get some good results. We had a 95% success rate in the first round of trials on mice, using a Kayl extract against MRSA."

"That's brilliant!" said Ward with a huge grin.

"We're proceeding with caution, but it's looking very promising."

Follow-up tests achieved similar results, with Kayl extracts showing efficacy against different strains of pathogenic bacteria and some viruses. Dose testing followed. "It has very low toxicity," observed Leeman, clearly impressed.

Leeman and his colleagues worked hard to perfect the formula. Ward learnt a lot along the way. By the time the drug was ready for human testing, they'd developed an oral preparation, and a low-dose topical formula with anti-inflammatory qualities. Subject to regulatory approval, the latter would be available over the counter on request. It was designed to treat stubborn skin infections, intended for everyday use, and showed promise against the symptoms of stubborn dermatitis, acne, and a number of unexplained sores and rashes. It was time for large-scale human testing to begin.

Chapter 4
Let Human Trials Begin

Terry went to the hospital with her overnight bag, followed signs through long stark corridors, and up some stairs. She felt uncomfortable and out of place. *Shit. What am I doing? I hate these places - sick people everywhere, pain and grief, not to mention animal testing, modern medicine...*

She stopped for a moment to gather her thoughts. *They think this will make me well. 'A miracle cure,' say the media. At least they're testing on me, this time. Not on animals.*

She continued tentatively, reached the Dermatology Clinic, registered at the desk, and took a seat as she waited for her consultant, Mr Singh, to call her through.

"Terry White." She heard her name called and looked across to see Mr Singh, "I can see you now," he said in a strong Indian accent. She got up and followed him into his consulting room.

"Do take a seat Miss White, how are you feeling today?"

"Nervous and in pain," she replied. "But hoping you can help."

"I hope so too! Tell me more."

"It was an effort just getting here. My sores were hurting. They do that when I walk too much".

"That sounds horrible. I see you've explored a lot of other treatments, with little benefit. Are you still keen to proceed with this new treatment?"

"Yes, definitely. It could be my last chance to live a normal life, free from pain, so I'm pinning a lot of hope on this opportunity."

"You said you were nervous. Is there anything in particular you're nervous about?" he asked.

"Well the sores are raw to touch, painful, and any kind of topical treatment stings like crazy. I'm a bit nervous about that. But apart from that, I'm just not a fan of hospitals. Hoping the treatment doesn't make things worse, I guess."

"OK. We'll begin cautiously. The Kayl antibacterial-antiviral cream that we're trialling has shown promising results on sores and rashes in the lab - it's anti-inflammatory too."

She nodded and listened carefully as Mr Singh explained the process and the risks. "We'll need to keep you in for a few days to monitor progress. It's not without risks. This is completely new. It has not been tested on people before. Allergic reactions are a real possibility, and there is also the chance that you'll receive a placebo as part of the double-blind trials. Are you sure you understand? "

"Yes," Terry said decisively. "I've got it all in writing, and I *do* want to proceed."

She signed a form relinquishing the consultant, the hospital, and the pharmaceutical company from any responsibility if anything went wrong.

"OK. If you're happy, I'll get a nurse to help you apply it the first time and then we'll monitor you over the next few days. Assuming all goes well, you can then self-administer at home, three times a day - morning, afternoon and evening." He smiled warmly, "I'll ensure you're monitored closely, so we can move quickly if you have a bad reaction."

She nodded, feeling optimistic. "Where do you want me?"

"Follow me," he said leading her to the changing rooms. He called a nurse, who stepped up to help. "This is Miss White who's taking part in our trials."

The nurse nodded. "Hello, I'm Nurse Keltz."

"Hi. You can call me Terry, if you like," she smiled faintly.

"Of course Terry. We'll be spending a bit of time together over the next few days."

Mr Singh started to move away. "I'll see you on the ward in a few minutes," he said as he marched off.

The nurse handed Terry a gown and she went to change, emerging a few minutes later with a pile of clothes under her arm. The gown flapped around, barely protecting her dignity, and her long, tousled hair fell loosely around her shoulders. She was pleased to see a clean white, starched bed waiting for her on the ward.

Mr Singh beckoned for her to sit on the bed. "Make yourself comfortable and Nurse Keltz will apply the first treatment. Then she'll come back to check on you regularly. You need to tell her if you feel anything is not right."

Terry hopped up onto the bed, wincing as a sore on her leg touched the sheets - it felt raw. "I really hope this stuff helps," she muttered as she got comfortable between the sheets. The nurse pulled the curtains around the bed, so they had privacy.

"Are you ready?" said Mr Singh.

Terry nodded, "Yes."

"Then I'll leave you to Nurse Keltz's expert care," he smiled and walked away.

But Terry's mind was in turmoil. *What am I doing? I've been opposing the pharmaceutical companies for years, and now I'm working with them. Is this the right decision? I've survived this long without drugs... but in pain, such pain. I so long to be better...*

"Can you show me which parts of your body are most affected at the moment?" Nurse Keltz interrupted her thoughts, while pulling on latex gloves.

"Um yes," she replied. *No chickening out now. This is a potential cure - just go for it girl!*

Terry tossed the sheet aside and pulled up her gown, pointing to a sore red area just above her left buttock, and a large rash running down her right leg. "That's been hurting a lot today," she said.

"Ooh I'm not surprised! That's nasty!" said the nurse, sympathetically. She twisted the lid off the tube of cream and gently rubbed the medicine into the problem areas.

"Ouch!" said Terry, gritting her teeth.

"Ooh sorry" said Nurse Keltz. She stopped for a moment. "Are you OK? Do you want me to continue?"

"Yes," she said, with tears in her eyes, "It just stings!"

The nurse continued for a while, until Terry yelped. Nurse Keltz turned to her, "Do you want to rest for a moment? Or are there other areas you'd like me to treat today?"

"Can we wait?" asked Terry. "See how I go? If there's no adverse reaction, you can do the rest?"

"That sounds very sensible," said the nurse. "I'll leave you to rest and pop back later."

"Thanks," said Terry calmly. She sat back and picked up a magazine to pass the time.

The nurse checked in on her a couple of times after that. "There's been no adverse reaction," Terry reported. "In fact, the cream is quite soothing after the sting subsides. Shall we complete the job?"

"OK. If you're happy with that," the nurse nodded.

Terry grinned, more relaxed now. "There's a rash on my foot and a nasty area on my scalp, which began as a sore, and then started bleeding a few days ago. I wonder if the sore got infected." Terry pulled her hair up to reveal a bleeding mess hidden beneath her dark curls. "It's not as painful as it looks, but it would be amazing to get rid of it," she said. "There's been no sign of scabbing. It just keeps getting worse."

"Oh my goodness, you poor love!" Nurse Keltz carefully applied the cream to the affected area, inevitably getting some into the patient's hair. Terry flinched with every touch. Then the nurse treated the rash on her foot. "Are we done?"

"I think so," said Terry.

"Now you should rest," said the nurse. "Let the medicine do its work, and let's hope you see all the benefits we expect, and more," she smiled. "Do you need a drink or anything?"

"I'm fine at the moment," replied Terry. She smiled and grabbed a book from her bag - The Rats by James Herbert, an old favourite and a modern classic. As she sank into the world of a rat-infested London, she started to drift off into a long, deep sleep.

Chapter 5
No Pain, No Gain

Morning dawned and Terry woke up, sat up in bed, and inspected her sores. *They're not as inflamed as yesterday.*

"I think it's working!" she called excitedly across the ward. Nurse Keltz rushed over, "Really? Let me take a look... Oh you're right... those rashes on your legs definitely look better. How's your head?"

Terry leaned over to show her. Nurse Keltz lifted her hair, "Well it's improving. No bad reactions?" Terry shook her head, "Then hopefully you're on the mend!"

"Fingers crossed," Terry grinned. The nurse pulled the curtains back against the wall, and Terry spotted a familiar figure loitering beside the ward door. "Charlotte?"

"Afraid so!" The woman walked briskly to her bedside. I heard you were in hospital and thought I'd call in - see if you need cheering up!"

"It's great to see you!"

"Well I've been a crap friend. Haven't been around for a while, but I thought you'd appreciate a visit."

"I do! Take a seat. How long has it been?"

Charlotte perched on a plastic chair. "At least a couple of years. Sorry for my tardiness staying in touch. I was in the area, tried to call at the house, and Alex said you were in hospital. Didn't seem very happy about it, but he told me where to find you. How are you?"

"He's not very happy... but I'm good. Hoping I might have found a cure for that persistent skin problem that's been plaguing me for years."

"Oooh goodie. That sounds like a turn up for the books! I remember you vanishing off the social scene when it flared up before. Not nice."

"It's been the bane of my life for the past decade. It'd be amazing if I can finally get rid of it."

"Too right. What's up with Alex? I remember you guys years ago, out on protests, waving banners. You were full of life and passion." She waved her arms jovially, emulating the protests.

"He's angry because he doesn't agree with the medical treatment I'm receiving," Terry said flatly. "I'm surprised he's still at the house - I thought he might have moved out by now. We're living separate lives."

"Oh no!" said Charlotte. "I thought you guys were the real thing! I thought you'd be together forever!"

"So did I!" said Terry. She adjusted her pillows and fiddled with her glass of water before taking a sip.

"I'm so sorry," said Charlotte.

"It's a pretty unpleasant atmosphere at home. Nice to be out of the house for a bit."

"That sounds horrible."

"It's like a war zone, but it's my house, my inheritance. Alex was never able to keep a job or stay out of prison long enough to get a place of his own. As you know, he was a bad boy - always taking things too far and getting into trouble with the law!"

Charlotte nodded. "Yes, I remember."

"I loved him though," Terry continued, "and our relationship worked... until now. He's very bitter. Living together in this atmosphere is pretty unbearable, but I'd still like to work it out, if the will's there."

"What a pity. I thought he was quite understanding."

"Well he was. That's the thing. The first time my skin broke out in sores and rashes, nearly a decade ago, I was inconsolable and Alex was great. A real comforter. He applied natural moisturisers liberally, gave me herbal anti-inflammatories, and offered other natural remedies to try to alleviate the pain."

"Did it help?"

"Not really. And that's the problem. There was a short period of improvement and then it got worse again. I hope that's not going to happen with my current treatment, but you just can't tell. Back in those days, I was in agony and couldn't move around without help. I needed nursing care. The pain was raw. I was pissing in a pot because sitting on the loo hurt, and the whole thing was humiliating."

"That's terrible." She gave Terry a gentle hug.

"Ooh mind the sore bits," she said good-humouredly. "Yes, It *was* terrible. I couldn't work when it was bad, but the symptoms would come and go, so I took casual work when I had a good spell. Then it would strike me down again out of the blue. Put me out of action for weeks. I'd have months of relative normality and then wake up to discover painful rashes on my body. Sometimes, it meant I was confined to bed. It's been a total curse! I'm only in my 30s - I should be in the prime of life!"

"What do the doctors say?"

"They don't know what's wrong with me. They've looked into allergies, environmental factors, and other possible causes. They keep drawing blanks and once they even suggested it was psychological. That made me mad, because it's not in my mind. I had raw skin, bubbling and peeling. I just thought they were idiots when they suggested it was psychological."

Charlotte rolled her eyes and gently took Terry's hand. "I had no idea you'd been through so much. Sorry I haven't been around more. Why this treatment now?"

"It's a new product, on a clinical trial," continued Terry. "The researchers were looking for people with 'untreatable' skin problems, hoping to offer something that could change lives. It's designed to destroy pathogenic bacteria, viruses and reduce inflammation, but I don't know if bacteria or viruses are the cause of my problem. Tests for microbial infections have always come back negative. That said, I've often wondered if there's something nasty that's evading detection.

"In the end, the doctors just wondered if the cream might benefit me. It's shown remarkable benefits on some unusual skin conditions, and I fitted the profile for one of their target patient groups. People for whom nothing else seemed to work. It's early days, but at the moment, this new medicine does seem to be helping. I hope it's not too good to be true!"

"Thank Goodness you've found some relief!" said Charlotte. "I hope it continues to work."

"I'm feeling very positive," said Terry. "Now tell me all your news!"

Charlotte stayed with her for a couple of hours, sharing her own stories, and catching up on old times. It was a welcome distraction.

"Sorry to interrupt, but it's time for your next treatment!" said Nurse Keltz.

"Oh that's fine. I need to get off anyway," said Charlotte. "I have to work this afternoon."

"Thanks for coming by," said Terry. "I really appreciate it." They waved goodbye.

Nurse Keltz pulled the curtains. "So, how are you doing now? Can I put the cream on again, and we'll monitor you for a couple more days. See how it goes?"

"Yes, please do. I've got a good feeling about this."

*   *   *

Terry felt a little better with every passing day.

"If you're happy to continue on your own, you can go home today," said Nurse Keltz.

Terry nodded, "OK."

"We'll need regular updates on your progress, and do let us know quickly if you experience any side effects. I'll fetch Mr Singh."

The consultant was happy with Terry's progress and she was discharged, full of anticipation, and energised with a new lease of life.

When she got home however, Alex was there and the atmosphere was thick with hatred and contempt. "How many animals were tortured and died grisly, painful deaths at the hands of lab technicians in the name of medicine?" he asked, "All because you had a few small rashes. Stupid cow."

She went from elation to tears in moments, "Oh please Alex, try to understand how badly I needed this treatment."

"You didn't need treatment! You've got by for years, learnt to live with it. You're selfish!" he scowled. You disgust me! I can't bear to look at you!"

"I was in pain!"

"So it's OK for animals to die in pain?"

"No. I didn't mean that."

"You contemptible woman. I cannot understand how your standards have fallen so far."

"Oh please try to understand Alex?"

But he wouldn't understand. He slept in the spare room for the rest of the week and they avoided one another.

Chapter 6
Fire Fire

Terry gazed out of the rear window of her home. Across the field was a farmhouse and a few barns. *This is such a lovely place to live. I feel blessed.*

Watching the country life relaxed her - the lambing in April, the milk being transported from the cow shed, the chickens running free-range around the farm. *Even that dastardly cockerel who won't let me sleep has grown on me,* she thought. *It's such a tranquil setting. So peaceful. Good for healing.*

The house overlooked an enchanting landscape, with fields as far as the eye could see. She looked out over a patchwork of greens, browns and yellows – in the far distance was a field of glorious red poppies. Cows and sheep grazed nearby.

I'd better get out into the garden - lots of weeds to get under control! Need to catch up with friends too. They'd been a lifeline while she was housebound during flare ups.

The illness had made her very dependent on Alex for company. It was irksome and lonely when he went to prison, but even more lonely, now he was angry and bitter, even though they were living under the same roof.

As she sat near the window, she reminisced on her former life... wondering if it was all behind her now. She snapped out of her thoughts. She needed to look forward not back.

*   *   *

That evening, Alex appeared in the doorway with a suitcase, "I can't stay here. You make me sick!" he said coldly. "I've got a mate who's prepared to put me up for a while. When you come to your senses, call me. Or don't. I don't care any more." He left.

Tears rolled down Terry's cheeks. *Why can't I have everything – both good health and the love of a man?* Just as one problem appeared to be have found a resolution, a new problem emerged: loneliness, heartache, and a terrible sense of loss.

Months passed, her physical wounds healed, and the pain of Alex's departure softened, but it still made her sad.

Charlotte called, "Come to the pub. Let's catch up." She didn't need to ask twice.

"How's life, now you've been out of hospital for a few months?" she asked.

"It's getting better with every passing day," said Terry. "I've got a new job, in a local shop. So far so good. The shop's very busy at weekends and I like the friendly bustling atmosphere. In the old days a busy shop would have been too much for me. It's nice to feel normal for a change, to do a full day's work, and catch up with people I haven't seen in a while!"

"That sounds great. I can't stand my job, but it pays the bills."

"What are you doing?"

"Office job. Admin. Crap pay, crap conditions, crap everything, but needs must."

"Oh, sorry to hear it's that bad."

The two women laughed. "Oh some day's it's not so bad," said Charlotte, "but it's not exactly fulfilling a childhood dream or anything. I'd like to move on to something that excites me one day."

"And what would that be?"

"Ahh that's the million dollar question, isn't it. I wanted to be a dancer when I was young, but wasn't allowed to join classes, so that dream fell by the wayside. I studied English and thought about being a journalist but couldn't get a break. I think charity work could be quite fulfilling. I don't have experience in that sector, but I think it's worth a punt. I'm keeping an eye on jobs coming up with some local charities. How about you?"

"I'm happy just working in the shop for now. I never really thought about a career path, because after school, I just wanted to get some money together and took the first thing that came along. Then I got ill, so it was harder to make plans. I'm trying to make up for it now - not so much with work, but by getting my social life back on track and trying to reconnect with people I haven't seen in a long time."

"I'll drink to that!" They clinked glasses and grinned. "To a better future!"

"How do you feel about Alex, now he's gone?" asked Charlotte.

"Honestly? I'm torn," said Terry. "I had to do something. The disease was ruining my life. But I've lost my soul mate, and alone at night, that's hard. I feel empty, incomplete, and just sad. But I try to keep busy and look forward to good times. You know how your darkest thoughts always come to haunt you at night? When you can't sleep? That's when it's hardest. There's a definite void, which Alex used to fill."

"You'll meet someone else when the time's right."

"I guess so."

"Another drink?"

"Why not."

As Terry drove home, she spotted flames and heavy smoke rising into the sky. *What's that? The farmer doesn't usually have bonfires. Is one* of his *barns on fire?*

Oh no! It's the thatched roof of my house!

As she drew close, she could see the fire brigade fighting the blaze. Bright orange flames leapt into the air. Gallons of water disappeared into her beautiful little home.

Tears rolled down her cheeks. She was in shock, distraught, devastated. She stopped in the road and watched as the horrors unfolded, almost in slow motion. It was surreal - like it wasn't really happening, but the acrid smell of smoke confirmed that it was very real and she ran to the scene.

"That's my house!" she stuttered to the nearest fireman. *I've lost everything.* Feelings of alarm, dismay, and utter devastation engulfed her. An emotional rollercoaster of horrible feelings overwhelmed her.

The firefighter took her aside, "We received a call from a passer by who saw the thatch simmering. By the time we arrived, the whole place was up in flames."

"How did it start?" she asked hopelessly.

"We don't know yet. We'll have to investigate and write a report when the blaze is out."

A police officer stepped in, "Are you the owner of this property?"

"Yes," she sobbed.

"I'll need to take your details. Do you have somewhere to stay for the night?"

"Erm… I don't know. I'll need to make some calls." She rang Sheila.

"Of course you can stay with me!" said Sheila. "You poor love."

Terry watched the firemen, still trapped in a weird bubble of surrealism peppered with disbelief. She hoped she'd wake up and find it had all been a nightmare. But it was real.

In the morning, Terry and Sheila went to survey the wreckage together. "It's a burnt out sodden shell," said Terry flatly. The walls were standing but the roof had collapsed and everything was black.

"Come on sweetheart," said Sheila, as she comforted Terry and led her away from the scene. "The insurance company will sort it out soon and then you'll have a clearer idea where you go from here. You can stay with me for as long as you need to. I know the flat's a bit cramped, but I enjoy the company. Let's go home, deal with the insurance claim, and try to sort things out."

Chapter 7
Man Hunt

A few days later, Terry's phone rang. "Hello?"

"Hello Ms White, It's WPC Taylor here."

"Is there any news?" asked Terry.

"We've heard from the fire service, and they say the fire was started deliberately," she explained. "Traces of petrol were found on the charcoaled thatch. Can we come by to ask you some questions?"

"Of course!" she said.

Half an hour later, WPC Taylor and her colleague, Inspector Dawson, were standing on the doorstep to the block of flats. They buzzed the intercom and went inside.

"Come in. Take a seat," said Terry. "Sheila's just making some tea."

"Thank you. I'm sorry to come in such unpleasant circumstances," said WPC Taylor. "We need to have a chat - see if we can identify anyone who might have a motive to start the fire. Is there anyone with a grudge against you Terry? Anyone who would wish you harm?"

Terry's mind was spinning and she couldn't think clearly. "I don't know," she stuttered, tears welling up in her eyes. "I don't get it. Why would someone start that fire deliberately? I don't have any enemies."

"That's what we're trying to find out," the WPC said sympathetically.

Her mind raced, trying to think of something useful to say. Anything. *Who would do something like that?* "It must be kids. Just stupid, dumb kids, looking for a thrill," she suggested, unable to come up with a better explanation.

The police officers looked at each other, unconvinced. "Think Terry. Think through your friends, acquaintances, and significant others. Have you upset anyone? Was there anyone who might have a reason to hold a grudge?"

Terry wiped her eyes, and thought through her recent connections — in recent weeks she'd renewed contact with old friends, and made new acquaintances at work, but nothing stood out. Before that, there was Alex. He wasn't a happy bunny, but he was a pacifist and he was just hurting. She understood that.

Terry told WPC Taylor about her new friendships, and the break-up with Alex. "He was angry with me, but he wouldn't resort to arson," she explained. "He uses peaceful methods of protest and values *all* life. He's passionate about his causes, but he's not violent."

"OK. I hear you. Tell me more," said WPC Taylor.

"Well, he's a decent man. If anything, he has higher morals than I do. That's why we fell out! He moved out a few months ago, calling me a hypocrite... and he was right. It was complicated."

"We've got time," said the officer, so Terry explained everything that had happened.

"OK. Thanks for being so honest. The fire department is gathering more evidence from the scene and we'll be asking around the neighbourhood for any witnesses. We'll need to speak to Alex. Do you know how we can contact him?"

Terry handed her his mobile number, "It's all I've got for him now. We haven't been in touch since splitting up. It seemed pretty final." As the police officers left the building, Terry turned to Sheila. "That was hard. I don't know if I should even have mentioned Alex. He's a good man. He wouldn't have done it."

"Try to relax love. I think you made that clear. It's up to the police to look into things now. I expect he'll be eliminated from their enquiries quickly."

Back at the station, the police saw things differently. "This Alex Turnbull is one to watch," said WPC Taylor. "He's been in and out of prison for years. Got major anger management issues. His phone's going to voicemail and his registered address is Terry White's house - the one that's gone up in flames. I'm going to check his phone and bank cards, see if we can track his movements. I'll get some posters put up in the area - perhaps someone's seen him. People don't usually disappear like this unless they're deliberately trying to avoid being found. Or unless they're dead, which seems unlikely."

Back at the flat, Terry's skin condition flared up. "It's the stress," she said to Sheila miserably. "It often flares up when I'm under a lot of stress." She applied the Smooth cream, which helped soothe the sores, and it settled down again in a few weeks. She fed back the results to Mr Singh, just as she did every time. The drug had given her a new lease of life. It was just a pity that everything else had fallen apart.

*   *   *

The man-hunt was on. Terry lived in a small community, so ruling out bored local kids playing with fire was easy. They were, for the most part, good kids, and those questioned had alibis. The police were determined to track down Alex, their prime suspect, who had both motive and a history of criminality. He was moving around, sleeping on friends' sofas, deliberately evading anyone's attempts to contact him. Then one day, he was spotted in a pub - the police were on site in minutes.

"I'm arresting you on suspicion of arson," said WPC Taylor, "You do not have to say anything. But it may harm your defence if you do not mention when questioned, something you later rely on in court. Anything you do say may be given in evidence."

At the station, he was led to an interview room and quizzed by officers.

"Where were you on the night of the arson?" asked WPC Taylor.

"At the cinema."

"On your own?"

"Yes."

"Can you prove that? Do you have a ticket? A receipt? A credit card statement? Or can someone vouch for having seen you there?"

"Not that I remember... It was weeks ago!" he was irritated.

"We'll need to verify your story and check the CCTV. Which cinema was it?"

"No comment. I want a lawyer."

"You can have a lawyer... but first tell us the name of the cinema."

"The big one on Turpin Road. I don't remember its name!"

"OK. We'll get that checked out."

"You can't keep me here!"

"We can keep you for questioning for 48 hours. We won't keep you longer than is necessary, Mr Turnbull."

That same night, WPC Taylor went down to Turpin Road Cinema to speak to the staff, show them a photograph, and get their CCTV recordings for the night of the fire. The video showed Alex turning up, just as he'd said, but not until after the blaze had started.

"I think he's as guilty as hell," she said to a colleague. "We had a witness come forward a few weeks ago reporting someone matching his description, who was sneaking around outside Terry White's house before it went up in flames. We need to organise an identity parade for tomorrow. I'm going to see if the shoes he's wearing match the prints found at the scene."

While Alex spent the night in custody, WPC Taylor and her team collected evidence against him. "He's going down," she said the next morning. "His shoes *do* match the footprints at the scene of the crime, and his fingerprints were found on a discarded petrol can nearby."

The evidence against him was compelling. He'd never been very good at covering his tracks. An identity parade the following morning sealed his fate - he'd been spotted sneaking around outside Terry's house, just before the fire.

"Alex Turnbull, I'm charging you with arson," said WPC Taylor, as they sat opposite one another in the interview room. Alex looked down, depressed. *Here we go again.* She handed him a charge sheet. "This sets out the details of the crime. You're still under caution. I'll leave you to speak with your legal representative."

Chapter 8
Getting High

Little Jessica, aged eight-and-a-half found this strange brown jelly in the garden fascinating. She liked jelly. Mum made it for parties and for puddings at the weekend. It was great when mum made it in a rabbit shaped mould – Jessica would consume the ears first and then the nose. Strawberry flavour jelly was her favourite, especially with ice cream.

Jessica looked intently at the brown jelly growing in the garden. *I wonder what this tastes like? It's brown... perhaps it tastes like chocolate.* She sniffed it, then nibbled. *It doesn't taste of much. Hmm... it has a curious slippery feel. I'm not sure I like it!* She nibbled a bit more, then threw it back on the ground from where it had come. She went inside to watch cartoons.

As she watched Tom and Jerry, Jessica started to feel giggly. The cartoon seemed funnier than usual, and she felt a little light headed. She crashed out on the sofa half way through and fell into a fantasy dream-world where mice were stronger than men, and cats worshipped rodents as kings.

"Jessica?" she was awakened from her slumber by a gentle push to her shoulder and her mum's soft tones. Mum looked concerned. "How come you're so tired? This isn't like you?"

Jessica smiled, "I don't know mum. I feel fine now."

It was a few days later at school when Jessica made the connection between her dreamy state and the jelly in the garden. There was a rumour going round school that this stuff was better than a *One Direction* concert for a guaranteed buzz. She wasn't sure about this. She'd never been to a *One Direction* concert.

It became the cool thing at school to get 'happy' on this jelly. It was free. It was natural. What could be the harm?

*   *   *

Little Jessica and her friends were making a habit of hiding out in the shed, nibbling the fungus, and falling into giggles. But it wasn't just them. Schools across the UK were finding themselves faced with a problem.

"The kids are coming into school in a daze," complained Jessica's English teacher in the staff room. "Some cannot concentrate properly. They're slipping into daydreams."

"I know," agreed a colleague. "The Headmaster's asked the caretaker to rake up all the fungus and remove it from the school grounds, but I think he'll be fighting a losing battle."

"It's so prolific!"

"Yes and the children have been told to leave it alone, but they're not listening."

"I guess they're just curious... But I'm worried it's harming their education and doing God-knows-what to their brains!"

"We're going to have to clamp down on those who continue to use the fungus."

"But how? It's impossible to control when it's so widespread across the neighbourhood!"

"I don't know. Some kind of test, accompanied by incentives to keep them off the stuff!"

"Oh, I don't know about testing. It's pretty obvious when someone's high from this stuff. I think we need a team meeting, to work out a plan."

It wasn't just children. Adults had discovered its mind-altering effects too, and given it the street name, *hot caffeine*. This legal high was becoming so widely available, that the traditional drug pushers were going out of business, and within a few short months, some bars had started selling washed, sliced, dried and flavoured packets of *hot caffeine* as a bar snack.

MPs were concerned about its safety. "A committee has been formed to look into the safety of consuming *hot caffeine*," announced the PM during Prime Ministers Questions. "The committee will also look at health and safety at work and whether we need to specifically ban driving or operating machinery under the influence."

"Well it's a start," murmured MPs in the House of Commons.

Talk shows and bars were alive with discussions about the substance. Should it be banned altogether? *How* could it be banned anyway, when it was growing in everyone's gardens?

29

Should consuming it be criminalised? More importantly, could a ban on consumption be enforced? How should schools be advised to deal with the problem?

There were many questions, and no easy answers when *hot caffeine* was so widely available, and becoming increasingly popular. There was a growing element of society enjoying its effects, and to add to the problems, they had formed a powerful lobby group to keep it legal. They had influential supporters in high places.

Chapter 9
Chillin'

Elsewhere, in a squat in East London, teens were spending all day getting high on *hot caffeine*.

"Hey man... you mellow?" said Mark to his buddy Kevin.

"Yeah man... this is the life."

Eighteen year old Mark had been living the highlife in an abandoned concrete block of flats since leaving home at 16. The building was derelict and supposedly unsafe, but he'd been squatting there for years and never had any trouble. "It's safe as houses. Solid as a rock," he'd say.

The area was dilapidated. No one showed much interest in it, and that was fine by him. Apparently there was asbestos in the building which put developers off the plot as an investment opportunity, and made it too expensive for the council to demolish. So it just stood there, creating an eyesore on the landscape. That suited Mark and Kevin nicely.

Mark had begun his life as a vagrant nicking food and stealing money to buy drugs. But that seemed like a loser's game once he realised he could get high all day long on this free stuff, which just grows in the ground everywhere!

His mates hung out playing music, talking about cars and girls, and all the things they aspired to, but were unlikely to ever achieve because they were wasting their lives in wretched squalor. It beat working in some dead-end joint all day, making someone else rich just to pay the rent.

This fungus was cool. Just a little nibble and you were away. It didn't take much.

Is it addictive? he wondered. *Who cares! It's free!* He relaxed into a cosy corner of the flat as he sunk into a strange utopia.

"D'ya s'pose this stuff's addictive?" he asked Kev later.

"Na mate. There's no downer. Just a sense of 'real life'. Boring. Depressing. Life."

Mark giggled, "The kind of life that's best avoided whenever possible".

"Yeah. Difficult. Stressful. Real."

Mark grinned.

The truth was, *hot caffeine* was mildly addictive and was definitely habit-forming. Heavy users might struggle to give it up, but no one was worried about that.

"Hey Kev – my toe nail's gone white and funny looking," he gazed down at his foot, holding his sock in the air.

"Mine too mate – happening to everyone. Just the way things are – nothing to worry about. Just chill."

So they chilled.

*   *   *

"Hey mum," said Jessica. "The supermarket's selling dried, flavoured packets of *hot caffeine!* Can we try some?"

"No Jess, it's not good for your education. You know what the school says. You shouldn't be nibbling it."

"Aw mum, everyone else is using it."

"Not everyone. Not those who want to get good grades!"

"Boring."

While not everyone was convinced, the fact that supermarkets were now stocking hot caffeine in different flavours, did give it a certain acceptability, and it became a normal 'feel good' snack at home. Anyone worried about the hygiene of eating it raw from the ground, felt happier about this processed product. It tasted good too. The intervention of food processing companies assured the public that the product on the shelves was safe to eat.

Hot caffeine was lined up along the alcohol aisle, labelled by flavour, sweetness, and saltiness. As a voluntary measure to address concerns in some sectors of society, the checkout assistants were told not to sell it to anyone under the age of 16.

*   *   *

Jessica had been nibbling on the stuff for about six months, despite protests from adults, when she noticed something a bit odd.

"Mum? My mouth's funny. My tongue's gone white and I don't like the taste," she grumbled.

"Let me have a look," said her mum, "Open wide – stick your tongue out. Say ahhh."

"Ahhhhh"

"Hmmm, I don't know. It looks a bit creamy, but not particularly unusual. Do you want to see what the doctor thinks?"

"Yuck! Don't like doctors!" said Jessica in disgust.

"Well we can leave it for now and see if it clears up. If you don't feel right in a few days – we can go to see the doctor."

"Hmm," Jessica slumped. "I want the taste to go away now."

"I'll grab some mouthwash from the supermarket – that should help. Fresh mint flavour suit you? Like Polo mints?"

That sounded nice! Jessica nodded and smiled.

The mouthwash tasted like sweets and Jessica gargled enthusiastically. She wanted to swallow but was under strict instructions to spit it out. The funny thing was though, it didn't clear the problem.

So a week later they went to see the doctor. Jessica sat in the waiting room, fidgeting and pouting miserably.

"Tell the doctor what the problem is," prompted mum in the doctor's office.

"It's here… ahhhh…" she pointed to her tongue, adding, "white and *disgusting!*"

"I think you have a touch of oral thrush," said the doctor, "It's nothing to worry about – just take these pastilles and they'll make it go away." The doctor smiled.

"You mean I eat sweets to make it go away?" Jessica was confused.

"They're special sweets – with medicine in them."

"OK," This sounded good to Jessica. She turned to mum, "Does that mean I can't have the mint flavour mouthwash any more?"

"Not at all – you can keep using it if you like – it might help to keep your teeth in good condition."

Special sweets and yummy drinks! This isn't such a bad affliction after all! thought Jessica.

Chapter 10
The Drug Trials

"How have you been Terry?" asked Mr Singh, at one of her regular follow up consultations.

"The treatment is going well," she said. "I've been really pleased with the results - it definitely helps my skin to heal. The problem does come back sometimes, and complete healing of a difficult area seems to take ages, but it's very reassuring to see visible improvement as I persevere."

"That's great news."

"Yes, it is. I'd be bouncing off the walls if everything else wasn't such a disaster."

"What's the disaster?"

"Oh, it's been a difficult time. My partner left me, then my house burnt down. It's taken a lot out of me."

"Oh, that's awful. I'm so sorry. Do you have somewhere to stay?"

"Yes, with a good friend, and the insurance company has been very understanding, so I'll be able to move into a new place soon. I don't want to outstay my welcome."

He nodded sympathetically. "And has that affected the treatment?"

"My skin condition worsened for a while - stress usually makes it worse. I tried to stay calm and continued with the treatment." She fiddled with her hair and looked thoughtful. "Overall, my condition improved in the longer term. It's just unfortunate that my life's a mess, because under better circumstances, I might have got better more quickly. I'm pleased with the results though. I can work, go out, and live a normal life, which wasn't always possible during flare ups before."

"That's good. No side effects?"

"No, I don't think so. It's the only thing in my life that has gone well."

He jotted down some notes and smiled. "Well I'm glad we're able to help."

"Will I be able to continue using the cream? Once the trials are complete? If I need to?"

"We'll see, There's plenty of time yet - we're looking into the effects of long term use. I'll need to take some blood tests to monitor what's going on in your body, liver function - that kind of thing."

"OK. Thank you."

He brought a nurse in to take bloods and sent Terry on her way with more medication to keep her going until the next review.

*   *   *

Terry's treatment was one of two new products going through clinical trials. She was trialling the cream. The second item was an oral antibiotic, containing the same active ingredients.

Mr Singh reported back to the drug company, Cother Pharmaceuticals: "Early results from patients taking part in my trial have been very promising. All my patients are being closely monitored for side-effects, but few have been reported." He appended the detailed data.

Leeman collated reports from different doctors involved in the trial. "It looks like the drug is going to be a huge success," he said to colleagues. "We've got some positive feedback from those taking placebos, which muddies the waters a little, but the visible improvements among those using the real drugs are much more dramatic. I'm really pleased. They're showing a lot of promise."

Across the UK, patients like Terry White, once disabled by their conditions, were experiencing a new lease of life.

Back at home, Leeman was talking to his wife Jenny, "These fungal extracts are truly remarkable. The results are exceeding all my expectations. We're seeing antibiotic-resistant bacterial infections killed dead by the powerful new drug.

"Sounds like a miracle cure!"

"It is! This will save lives. I reckon we're onto the biggest medical breakthrough of the 21st century, although I guess it's early days! We have a lot of research still to do, but there's so much potential for this medicine. It's really exciting."

She gave him a huge hug and he grinned from ear to ear.

The trials enabled Leeman and his team to work out optimal doses, identify precisely how well each drug worked for different complaints, and to identify other possible clinical applications and areas for further research.

The results were published and praised across the medical world. Competitors undertook their own research on the medicinal qualities of Kaylmycotopa, but Leeman and his team were miles ahead. As the first person to formally identify the curative qualities of Kaylmycotopa, he won the Nobel Prize in Medicine.

"This is the proudest moment of my life," he beamed as he accepted the award. "But I can't take all the credit — I've had amazing support from my research team and from my wife, who has endured my long hours and late nights in the lab."

David Leeman was fast gaining a public profile, a degree of celebrity status, and all the ups and downs that go with it. It was surreal.

Chapter 11
The Criminal Trial

Alex's trial date came.

"You are charged with one count of arson. How do you plead?"

"Not guilty."

The prosecution set out the evidence. Dr Paul, a Police forensic expert took the stand. "We've matched fingerprints from a petrol can found at the scene, with the defendant," he said. "His shoes matched fresh footprints found outside the house on the night of the fire, and we have a witness who picked the defendant out of a line-up. She'd seen him sneaking around the house after dark, just before the fire began." The evidence against Alex was compelling.

The witness was called to the stand to recount what she saw. "He was holding something - it seemed heavy and clumsy. His behaviour was strange. That's why I noticed it, and remembered it. I guess the heavy thing he was carrying was a petrol can."

"Objection!" shouted the defence lawyer. "That is pure speculation!"

"Objection sustained," said the Judge. The witness answered questions and then stepped down.

The Chief Fire Officer took the stand. "We found evidence of petrol on the charcoaled thatch, indicating that the fire was started deliberately," he explained, and as he elaborated on their findings, the evidence for arson was almost irrefutable.

Experts and witnesses gave more evidence, and by the end of the trial, they'd proved beyond any reasonable doubt, that Alex was at the scene of the crime - but was it just circumstantial? It didn't look that way. The prosecution decimated his character. Witnesses were called up to show that he'd had a life-long anger management problem. His long list of previous convictions were scrutinised. Then Terry was called to take the stand.

"Tell me about the time you were admitted to hospital with multiple injuries after Alex Turnbull came home on weekend leave from prison," said the prosecuting barrister.

Terry looked sheepish, "I upset him."

"You upset the defendant?"

"Yes."

"So what did he do?"

"He set me straight. He corrected me."

"He beat you to the point that you needed medical attention. Isn't that right?"

"Yes." She whimpered quietly.

"Please speak up Miss White. The jury needs to be able to hear you."

"Yes," she said more loudly, tears welling up in her eyes, "But I shouldn't have upset him."

"The hospital report says you were admitted with a black eye, severe bruising, and a fractured jawbone. That must've been painful and taken a long time to heal?"

She nodded.

"Please speak up Miss White."

"Yes," she said.

"Yet despite that, you still stayed with him?"

"That was a one off. He was good to me most of the time. We had a lot in common. I loved him."

"Thank you Miss White."

As the evidence mounted against Alex, his barrister advised him to change his plea to 'not guilty by virtue of diminished responsibility'. "You've got psychologists' reports dating back decades about the effects of PTSD on your behaviour," he reminded Alex.

"They say you have suppressed rage caused by childhood abuse, and while mostly you live with the trauma, suppressing it, betrayal from a loved one just pushed you over the edge, causing a moment of rage - temporary insanity. We should argue that your suppressed rage triggered a bad reaction and that needs treatment, not more jail time."

Alex looked defeated. "Is that really my best defence?"

"I think so, but it's up to you."

"OK," Alex agreed to change his plea.

"My client needs help with his anger management issues, to help him respond more appropriately to overwhelming experiences in the future. Incarceration clearly hasn't rehabilitated him successfully in the past," argued the defence lawyer. "It's unlikely to help him become a better person in the future. There's a simmering rage, caused by childhood abuse, which can be treated and *should* be treated, so he is no longer a threat to society upon his release."

After much deliberation, Alex's plea of diminished responsibility was accepted. He was sent to a secure hospital for an indefinite period.

*   *   *

"The insurance company's finally sorted out interim payments for alternative accommodation," said Terry to Sheila. "I can get out from under your feet now."

"Oh there's no rush dear," said Sheila. "I enjoy the company!"

"That's very kind," said Terry. "But I should get my own place. They still need to process the other paperwork and sort out what else they owe me, but at least it's progress." She sat in the flat, watching the news on TV. *Hot caffeine* was the issue of the day. Politicians were worried about it, young people were deliriously happy about it, and stuffy old people were disapproving. Terry? She was just glad to be cured from her affliction - or at least have a treatment to hand when it flared up. She didn't care what anyone else did.

Cameras zoomed in on Doctor Jenkins, from the London University Research Centre: "The Kaylmycotopa fungus continues to thrive in our communities," he said. "Some organisations have attempted to ban its consumption at work, while operating machinery, or in school, but many such bans have had little effect. It's almost impossible to control because it's freely available and grows all around us in the damp warming climate.

"I'm on the government committee investigating the effects of *hot caffeine* as a recreational drug, and we're concerned that people are not taking the risks seriously. *Hot caffeine* is known to inhibit your ability to concentrate in the short term, and the long-term effects are still being studied."

"What other effects do you know about?" asked the reporter.

"Well, the combination of *hot caffeine* and alcohol leads to quicker drunkenness, and public bars are offering dried *hot caffeine* in different flavours. Some research suggests that the consumption of *hot caffeine* has outstripped that of alcohol. It's become a socially acceptable relaxant and alcohol sales have fallen because people are switching, or using both. Combining the two drugs presents an unknown risk to health.

"What's your view on the chocolate-coated *hot caffeine* available in supermarkets, which specifically targets children?

"That's just fundamentally wrong. This stuff can be quite potent and we know it's habit forming. It's not right to market it to kids."

"So are you taking action on that?"

"Yes. We're calling on the government to ban children from being able to buy *hot caffeine* in supermarkets. The voluntary arrangement of selling it to over 16s doesn't seem to be stopping youngsters from getting hold of it, so making this a legal obligation would be a step in the right direction. We don't know the long-term effects on human health, or on child development."

"That sounds very sensible," said the reporter.

"We'd like to see sales of the processed *hot caffeine* products in shops and bars taxed, like alcohol, to discourage excessive consumption among all users," he concluded.

"That's given us a lot to think about. Thank you for your time."

He nodded, "Thank you."

"Back to the studio."

In the newsroom, they continued on the topic. "It's a divisive issue," said the newsreader. "People hold strong views on both sides of the debate. Some lobby groups fighting against *hot caffeine* argue that its mild hallucinogenic effects could lead to psychosis with long-term use. Others say its calming effects are badly needed at a time when the country is overwhelmed by high levels of anxiety and mental illness. Dr Thom is here to tell us more."

Dr Thom quickly put down his glass of water and started to speak. "Yes, it's certainly a hot topic - and not one that's going to go away. The government has committed extra funding to researching the effects of the drug, and will be running a public awareness campaign of the known risks," he explained. "They hope to encourage a voluntary reduction in the consumption of *hot caffeine*.

"The short-term recommendation from the Department of Health is to stop consuming *hot caffeine*, at least until more is understood about its effects on the human body. It's wise to avoid operating machinery while under the influence, and to dissuade your children from indulging. The scale of the problem is being monitored, and a full report with solutions will be published in due course. In the meantime, the government plans to criminalise driving while under the influence of *hot caffeine*. A public awareness campaign will make sure the new law is widely known and police forces will be doing spot checks around the country."

The camera cut back to the newsreader. "We've got Lindsey Miller in the studio. She supports the use of the drug and is campaigning to keep it legal."

The camera cut to Lindsey. "We had an epidemic of mental health problems a few years ago," she explained, "but since *hot caffeine* became popular, people have been more able to relax. They don't feel so anxious or overwhelmed." She paused thoughtfully.

"Do you have any statistics on that?" asked the interviewer.

"Oh yes. Diagnoses of stress, anxiety, and depression have fallen hugely, about 90%. Stress-related prescriptions are at an all-time low. People are self-medicating with *hot caffeine* instead, and it takes away their worries and makes them feel good again."

"But aren't you worried that it might be detrimental to health in the long term?"

"No. Stress is bad for health, anxiety is bad for health. *Hot caffeine* doesn't have side effects like antidepressants, and frankly, it works better. I used to have chronic anxiety, but *hot caffeine* helps me relax. It helps me keep things in proportion."

"That's great for you. But what about children using the drug?"

"Children need to relax too. The levels of child mental health problems were growing before *hot caffeine* started growing in gardens. Now there's less conflict among society at large - people of all ages are getting on better. Stress levels have fallen, amongst all age groups. People are better able to cope with demands in their lives. It's a godsend. I cannot understand why anyone would want to go back to the way things were!"

Back to the newsroom. "So, as you can see, proponents of the drug argue that *hot caffeine* is relaxing, it reduces stress. Some say it makes them more creative – all of which is good for their health and good for society at large. Before *hot caffeine* became popular, the number of people taking time off work for stress-related illness was at an all time high. That number has now fallen dramatically. The debate continues."

Terry flicked the TV off. She wasn't a regular *hot caffeine* user, although she'd taken it from time to time. It felt good.

The Kayl jelly fungus that people called *hot caffeine* was used in foods and medicines, taken as a legal high, and used as a play thing by bored children. Most people weren't worried. After all, it was natural, it was free, it was turning a stressed-out society into a happy one – what could be the harm in that?

Chapter 12
Two Years On...

"Two new medicines will soon be available on the NHS," reported BBC News. "A new oral antibiotic, hailed as a 'panacea', will mark the end of antibiotic-resistant bacteria, after demonstrating incredible results in clinical trials. A topical cream, branded 'Smooth' will be available in clinic or over the counter. Its low dose of active ingredient is considered safe for personal use, without a prescription."

"That treatment has been amazing for me," said Terry, as she flicked off the TV. "Want a coffee?"

"Yes please," said Charlotte.

Terry filled the kettle and switched it on.

"So the treatment's continued to work for you then?" Charlotte asked.

"Oh yes. I've been clear from sores and rashes for a full two years, on and off. It's helped me enormously. Occasionally my skin flares up but I just treat it and carry on. Smooth has transformed my life. I used to be virtually disabled at times, but now I feel free as a bird!"

"That's amazing."

"It is. I had an ethical dilemma about it at the start, but now I'm just so pleased to have been part of the process that will change so many more lives."

*   *   *

The oral antibiotic quickly became used as a first line of defence against bacterial infections, widely prescribed by general practitioners and MDs. Its track record was so good - swift and efficient - it was even used for mild infections.

The brand name Smooth was chosen for the cream because it left people who'd previously been suffering from sores, rashes, unexplained blisters, boils, or dry flaky skin, with soft smooth skin

- something that obviously delighted many users. Beauty magazines posted rave reviews.

"Since its launch, Smooth cream has sold like hot cakes," wrote Cosmopolitan. "The benefits to women seeking relief for troublesome skin conditions have been nothing short of amazing. For effective relief from unpleasant dermatological conditions, it's definitely something to discuss with your doctor."

After gaining approval from the licensing and regulatory authorities in the UK and the United States, the medicines were rolled out across the world.

Word spread of its effectiveness, through case studies in the media and word of mouth. It became hugely popular, and a topic of excited conversation. Demand surged, exceeding manufacturing capability at times, with short delays and limited supply adding to the hype surrounding the 'miracle' product. Competing products moved in to take advantage of market forces, but Cother Pharmaceuticals held the patent, and competing products were poor imitations - they were simply not as good. A new factory opened to meet demand for 'Smooth'.

Terry was a total advocate. There was this weird thing though – she kept getting this irritating fungal infection on her skin. She treated it with antifungals, but it kept coming back. These things did have a reputation for being persistent and annoying. It was itchy and embarrassing. *Something to do with hormones*, she thought, and persevered with the antifungal treatments. She wasn't alone.

While many persistent and annoying skin conditions had responded very well to treatment with Smooth, one thing physicians across the western world were noticing was a growth in the volume of fungal infections. Smooth was useless for treating these infections. It had anti-viral and anti-bacterial qualities, but fungi were a different species of microbe altogether. Resistant and increasingly aggressive.

Superficial infections like thrush, athlete's foot, and cutaneous candidiasis - minor but irritatingly persistent - were becoming more common and more difficult to treat. Doctors shrugged it off. No one took fungal infections seriously - unless you were immunocompromised, and then it could be serious. It was a puzzle though. Why were they suddenly seeing so many more prevalent, persistent, and difficult to treat fungal infections?

One radical doctor, Dr Quinn, from California spoke out. "I'm telling you, the rise in fungal infections is caused by the widespread use of the new antibiotic drugs!" He was quite insistent, but his views were widely dismissed. All *real* doctors knew that people's healthy bacteria repopulated quickly after a dose of antibiotics. Anyone who thought otherwise was a nutter. Some medics conceded that a mild fungal infection was a possibility following a particularly long course of antibiotics, but they insisted it was easy to treat, which was not the experience of many patients.

Dr Quinn went on to suggest that the recreational use of *hot caffeine* might be another factor in the growth of fungal infections.

"Utter drivel!" said one of his peers, as they all jeered and ridiculed his ideas. "I should think he's consumed too much *hot caffeine* himself, to come up with such garbage." There was a roar of laughter. "His theories are not credible, there's no evidence, and frankly, I'd say he's gone a bit woowoo." The jibes and put-downs continued. He was considered eccentric and misguided by many mainstream medics, but gained a cult following of fascinated hippies.

* * *

Alex decided that his psychiatric ward was no better than jail.

"At least in jail you get a limited sentence. An end date. Something to look forward to," he grumbled to the elderly resident next to him, who had been there for decades. Stuck in here, I don't know whether they'll ever consider me well enough to leave.

"Beats a life sentence for murder," said the old man.

"I didn't kill anyone, I just burnt a house down."

"Yeah, but you could've killed someone in the fire – then it might have been murder."

Alex went off in a huff. "I want to go for a walk," he said to a nurse.

"When there's someone available to take you out, you can go. I'll put in a request," she replied.

He grumbled some more and sat down. *Life here is shit. We're drugged up most of the time. Don't feel anything much. But it's bloody dull, boring, frustrating. I want my life back.*

45

The food was overcooked and tasteless, the facilities were clinical and if you weren't mad when you went in, you'd be driven to insanity after a few months inside.

"I'm gonna get out of here!" Alex called over the humdrum, "You wait and see! If I can prove that I'm better, they'll have to let me out. 'Care in the Community' it's called. I'm going to show them I'm good to go."

"Are you taking your sedatives?" asked a nurse, "You shouldn't be this lively."

Alex quietened. He'd stopped taking them weeks ago, pretending to swallow them, then spitting them out and flushing them down the toilet. He didn't like the physical side effects – dry mouth, nausea, dizziness, headaches – and he didn't like the emotional numbness they caused.

"You know I have," he retorted quietly, and returned to his quarters like a well-behaved patient.

The absence of drugs gave him a new lease of life, and although he was acting sedated for the benefit of the medical staff, he was keen to escape from this hell-hole forever, given half the chance. As it happened, he didn't have to wait long. The culture of sedation meant that rules were pretty lax as no one was considered a threat.

An hour later a nurse came by, "Richard can take you out for a walk if you still want some fresh air?" she offered. Alex nodded, "Yes please," and followed her to the door.

"Wait here," she said. He did as he was told. Richard, a stocky no-nonsense black man, arrived.

"I hear you're keen to get outdoors?" he smiled.

"I just need some fresh air and a bit of exercise," Alex replied.

"Come on then – give me your hands, you know the rules." Alex gave Richard his hands. Handcuffs went on, and Richard unlocked the door.

The two strolled across the lawns.

"What did you do for a living before being sent here?" asked Richard.

"Oh, this and that," said Alex, "Odd jobs, casual labour – whatever came up. I was a full-time activist really – fighting for animal rights and the environment. No one takes climate change seriously enough. It's the biggest threat to human existence but

46

governments are more worried about company profits than the state of the planet."

An astute observation for someone better known for his violent temper and lack of compassion, thought Richard.

"I hate people," Alex continued, "People are destroying the world, and the innocent animals that depend upon the planet – they cage them in laboratories, torture them for medicine, and why? Money. It's all to increase company profits."

An extreme view. Perhaps the view that got him here in the first place.

"Do you talk to your psychiatrist about the way you feel?"

"Yes, but she thinks it's all in my head. It's not in my head. This stuff is real and it's happening right now. Most people just don't care and are happy to go along with the status quo."

Alex continued to vent his frustrations. It seemed his anger management therapy was having little effect – the cruelty and injustices of the modern world riled him. After twenty minutes Richard said, "Let's go back inside now. I have things I need to get on with."

"I don't want to go back inside! I'm sick of that place."

"Are you taking your sedatives?" Richard asked.

"You know I am!"

"Come on then," he took Alex's arm and led him back towards the hospital. Alex lashed out with his handcuffed arms, knocking Richard to the ground. He started running – no plan in mind, just wanting to feel free for a little longer. Then he stopped for a moment, realising that Richard had knocked his head on a concrete slab and was out cold.

Oh shit! For a moment he felt panic rising, then he realised the opportunity that lay before him. Grabbing Richard's keys, he removed the handcuffs and ran. The estate had high fences with barbed wire, and as Alex climbed them, he blocked out the pain of sharp needles piercing his skin. Leaving a trail of blood, he scrambled across the ten foot fence to freedom in the outside world.

He ran to the main road, limping and dripping with blood. He'd really hurt his leg on the barbed wire. He tried to hitch a ride. A car stopped briefly, but the driver took one look at his blood-stained institution clothes, and sped off. Eventually, he stepped out in front of an elderly driver, forcing him to stop, and quickly found himself a seat on the passenger side.

"To the railway station please!" he grinned a menacing grin at the poor old man, who didn't dare to argue, and did as he was told.

Alex abandoned his reluctant taxi at the station as a train pulled in, heading for London. He ran through the station, pushing other passengers aside, burst through the ticket barriers and jumped on the train for London, startling staff and passengers as the doors closed behind him. A sigh of relief escaped his lips as the train departed, eventually dropping him in the capital, where he slipped through the barriers, undetected amongst the crowds, and vanished onto the busy streets.

Chapter 13
On the Run

Alex was on the run. He came to a boarded-up former maternity hospital that had been closed for some time and had fallen into a state of disrepair. He climbed over the railings, and fought his way through the overgrown shrubs to a fire exit, where he forced his way in. Frankly, it wasn't that difficult – rot from the wooden door fell aside, making access easy. He pushed past dusty incubators that had clearly been out of use for years. Beyond that, another ward had rows of beds for the mothers.

This will do, he thought. *A bed for the night.* But as he lay there, trying to sleep, dust irritated his lungs, he coughed, shivered, and got up to find more blankets to protect him from the incessant cold.

The hospital made his room on the psychiatric ward look cosy, but this was temporary – and it represented freedom. No one was around and it felt like a safe place to hide. His wounds hurt, but he was exhausted. He eventually drifted off, into a deep sleep.

In the morning, he woke feeling stiff. Everything ached. He tried to move, and felt pain sear up his leg. His wounds stung. He winced in pain as he lowered himself off the bed and hobbled to a store room, where he found wet wipes. Sitting on the edge of the nearest bed, he wiped his wounds, cleaning up the blooded skin. Fresh bandages from a first aid kit enabled him to wrap some wounds - at least now they could heal. He hobbled to a wheelchair, lowered himself into it gently, and wheeled himself down the long halls of the hospital, where he peered through the gloom, trying to get a feel for his surroundings. The windows were boarded up, but a little light seeped through. Large cracks in the ceiling raised questions about the building's structural integrity.

A quiet scuffling sound broke the silence. Alex turned sharply as a rat emerged from an office and disappeared down the hallway.

He breathed a sigh of relief. There was something about this place that gave him the creeps.

He turned the wheelchair around and headed back down the hall, but as he turned a corner, two burly men confronted him, glaring, red faced and angry. His heart started beating so fast it felt like it was going to burst right out of his chest.

"What're you doing here?" one of them demanded. His switchblade glistened as it caught the light from a small broken window. These guys didn't look like executives from the local health authority.

Alex didn't answer. He felt beads of sweat forming on his forehead as his mind raced. *What do I say? Shit. They're gonna kill me.*

"Answer you imbecile!" the other man yelled.

"I'm in hiding," the weak and feeble reply slipped from Alex's mouth.

"Oh yeah?" he sneered, "From what?"

Alex felt horribly vulnerable. *Three years trapped in a psychiatric ward is a real killer for your confidence. I used to handle these situations so much better. People used to be afraid of me!*

The armed man did not look amused, but his partner looked highly entertained by the situation. "Are you deaf? You're hiding from what?" he asked again, impatiently.

"The authorities," Alex's faint words seemed to stick in his dry throat.

"You mean the cops!" he grinned.

Alex looked down at the vinyl floor, wishing desperately that it would open up and swallow him.

"Look at us, you pathetic little worm!" he demanded angrily, all amusement gone.

Fleeting thoughts sped through Alex's mind. *I wouldn't be in this position if Terry hadn't dobbed me in to the police and been a witness for the prosecution.* Rage overtook him and suddenly he felt ready to take these two monsters on. He looked up at the armed man, rose from his wheelchair, gritted his teeth to block out the pain, and sprung at him, taking him by surprise and knocking him to the ground.

The other man grabbed Alex, overpowered him, and threw him forcefully against the wall. Alex screamed – his wounds raw. The impact tore them open and blood seeped through the bandages. He got a new head wound to match. His whole body throbbed with pain. The men pulled Alex forward again, smashing his skull against the wall for a second time. Alex slid down the wall, a weak groan escaping from his lips.

"Let me finish him off," said the man with the knife, ready to slit his throat.

"No, leave him now. He won't trespass on our patch again."

He picked Alex up, and dragged him out to the car park, "Now pick yourself up, leave our patch, and find another place to hide. We own this estate and everything on it. You ain't welcome."

Alex was barely conscious, but he managed to pick himself up and crawl out of sight, before collapsing in some bushes and blacking out.

*   *   *

When he came to, it was dark. He was in a comfy bed.

Where am I? he thought. His head was pounding in pain. *Hang on a minute – what's this on my head?* He felt bandages.

His whole body hurt from the violence and the barbed wire. He'd never been so battered and bruised in his life. As he lay conscious through the harrowing pain, he thought about what had led to this situation in the first place – those clinical trials and Terry's betrayal.

The sound of footsteps interrupted his thoughts. He looked up in the dim light. It was a nurse. *Not another bloody institution!* he thought.

"Are you in pain?" she asked, voice hushed, trying not to wake everyone. He nodded.

"Everywhere hurts."

"I'll get you some pain killers and we can talk some more in the morning," she said.

The pain killers helped and he drifted off to sleep.

He awoke early in a panic. He couldn't stay here! They'd find him and take him back to that hell-hole. He clumsily tried to flee his bed, getting his foot caught in the sheets and landing face down on the floor. A nurse rushed over and helped him back into bed.

"You poor love, you must be so confused. Let me grab my papers, I need to ask you a few questions."

Questions? He didn't like the sound of questions.

She was back in no time, "What's your name?"

He looked blank. "I don't know," he mumbled. *I'm not bloody telling you my name!*

"Oh dear. Amnesia. We'll have to keep an eye on you. So I guess you don't know where you're from or who your next of kin is either then?"

He sighed and shook his head. *I can't stay here too long, or they'll get onto missing persons and then the cops will find me. Shit! What if the psychiatric nurse, Richard, died of his head injury? Then they'll do me for murder. I'm fucked! I gotta go.*

"You seem anxious," she said.

"I'm just confused," he said. "Not too keen on hospitals, if I'm honest. When can I leave?"

"You have some nasty wounds. It's going to take time to mend, get you feeling better, and to find somewhere for you to go. Hopefully your memory will return too. Try to be patient. We'll take good care of you," she spoke gently, smiled down at him, and then walked away.

He settled down to rest, while he worked out a plan. Soon breakfast was served. *Urgh! It's like the slop they served up in that hell-hole. I won't be sorry to see the back of hospital food when I get out of here!*

By evening, some of the wounds were starting to scab over. Everything felt a little less raw. Painkillers stopped his head from hurting too much, but his face wasn't a pretty sight. A policeman called in and the Ward Sister took him into her office.

Oh shit! Is this it? thought Alex, but the policeman left the building, and Alex settled into another restless sleep. The nurse was right. His wounds were bad. Leaving too quickly would jeopardise his recovery, but he was none-the-less nervous. Another 48 hours passed and he felt he was on the mend.

"I want to discharge myself," he said to the nurse, "I'm feeling much better and don't want to be taking up a bed unnecessarily."

"But you have amnesia! And you're still wounded. We need to identify you, ensure you have somewhere to go. And you'll feel worse when the painkillers wear off!"

"I'm fine," he insisted, as he pulled on his clothes and started towards the door.

"You can't just leave," she insisted. "You have to sign a form."

"So get me a form."

She scuttled off and returned before he could make himself scarce, "I don't think you should leave sir. We don't know who you are, and you're clearly not right. If you sign this, it's against medical advice."

"Give it here," he snarled, irritated, and grabbed the form from her hand. He signed it, 'Mickey Mouse'. "Now let me be." He left the building, still wrapped in bandages, but keen to secure his freedom once more.

The sense of relief as he walked free and unafraid for the first time in years, was immense. The wind rushed through his hair - cold but wonderful. His headache twinged but he tried to block it out. His wounds would continue to heal if he was careful. He breathed in the taste of freedom - the exhaust fumes and the flowers - scents and feelings that assaulted his senses in a way he'd dearly missed.

But as he walked through the streets of London, eyes darting and fearful of capture, the moment of elation passed. He shouldn't need to be afraid. He *should* be free. Anger and turmoil filled his being. His mind raced with the events of recent years - Terry, the fire, his custodial sentence, and the growing celebrity status of the man behind the drugs, David Leeman.

Nobel Prize winning prick! Leading figure in animal torture and vivisection. The man directly responsible for brainwashing Terry to abandon her principles and take part in clinical trials. He's the person ultimately responsible for landing me in an institution. Bastard. Where does he live I wonder? Revenge will be sweet.

He smiled.

Chapter 14
A Growing Problem

The radio played in the shop where Terry worked. One of the ads had a familiar ring. Music jingled and an actor said, "Problem skin? No problem! Speak to your doctor about Smooth skin cream. This award-winning cream has shown remarkable results, effectively treating a wide range of skin complaints."

"Bit of a miracle cure," said a customer, as she popped her goods onto the shop counter.

"What? Smooth?" said Terry.

"Yes. It got rid of my rosacea quickly and I've never looked back!"

Terry smiled. "I've had good results with it too."

"Ahh, you know what I mean then!"

Terry nodded and they both smiled.

Terry rung up the goods, took the money, and waved the customer goodbye as she left the shop.

The product's success seemed unstoppable - word of mouth recommendations boosted demand and increased people's confidence in the new drugs. New production plants met soaring demand around the world.

"The UK is now a world leader in pharmaceutical research and development," said the Prime Minister. "Britain is on the world stage. After years of being eclipsed by American advances in medicine, we're proud to claim our place in medical history."

Politicians of all parties were revelling in the euphoria, each trying to take credit for the good work achieved. None of them had actually done anything, apart from make supportive noises and turn a blind eye to tax loopholes, but details like that didn't matter. It was all spin.

"It's the biggest medical breakthrough since penicillin," the PM continued. "We've taken medical science a huge step further in the battle against dangerous microbes. These new products have created new jobs, boosted the economy, and enhanced our global reputation. We've put the 'Great' back into Great Britain!"

MPs and government officials patted themselves on the back, blissfully unaware of a problem brewing, and the challenges that lay ahead.

*   *   *

There was a theory within the alternative medicine community that the alarming growth in fungal infections seen in the western world, was caused by a combination of factors - unhealthy lifestyles, global warming, obsessive hygiene coupled with antibacterial products, and far too much cultural dependency on pharmaceutical drugs, rather than on preventative health. David Leeman started to wonder if Dr Quinn - who argued that the rise in fungal infections was caused by the new antibiotics and popular use of *hot caffeine* - might have a point.

The views of these radicals riled many medics, but Leeman could see some validity in their arguments. Global warming was undoubtedly a key contributory factor in the explosive growth of the fungus, Kaylmycotopa, which had led to the medical breakthroughs in the first place.

"I'm genuinely concerned," he told his wife Jenny privately. "I think Dr Quinn's theory might be right. If you consider that antibacterial products could conceivably compromise people's immune systems, by destroying healthy bacteria, then antibacterial soaps, wipes, and antibacterial drugs, could all be contributing to the rise in fungal infections. Combine those things with a warming climate and increased humidity, and conditions could be perfect for fungal infections to thrive and spread."

"I thought people recovered quickly after antibiotics and the microbial environment returned to normal."

"Well that's the prevailing medical belief, but what if they're wrong? What if people's healthy bacteria do NOT recover quickly following a course of antibiotics? There's research available that doesn't agree with this. It's not a view that's gone unchallenged. A superficial fungal infection is quite common among people who've been on a prolonged course of antibiotics.

"OK. It's an interesting theory," said Jenny.

"I just wonder if our new antibiotics might be contributing to the problem. Antibiotics destroy healthy, immune-boosting

55

bacteria, which would normally provide some protection against pathogenic fungi."

"The western world was addicted to antibiotics before you came along."

"True, but still..."

"You're uncomfortable."

"Yes."

"So take it to the board and do some research to find out if the theory is correct."

"I'm not sure they'll want to pursue that line of enquiry."

"Well you can ask."

Leeman approached the board of Cother Pharmaceuticals, to request funding to study the outbreaks of fungal infections and what might be causing them.

"As you know, fungi are resistant to the antibiotic drugs," he explained. "So the drugs kill bacteria, but not pathogenic fungi in the human body. Our bodies contain a delicate balance of microorganisms, including healthy bacteria, yeasts, and fungi, which are usually harmless. Our good bacteria keep the other microbes in check and help prevent disease.

"But there's a microscopic battleground in our guts, where our population of healthy bacteria fends off disease-causing microbes competing for a dominant position. It's healthy bacteria, supported by our immune system, that protects us from many infections.

"So now there's been an outbreak of fungal infections," he held up pictures of some of the more visible infections, where white patchy fungal infections had caused lesions on the skin.

"I want to investigate possible causes. The success of our antibacterial products has been great for destroying disease-causing bacteria, but it has also killed a lot of healthy microbes. This compromises people's immune systems in the short-term. It's possible it's contributed to the increase in fungal infections."

"You are joking?" said the Chair of the board "This could destroy our reputation! We're not responsible for the fungal outbreak, and we certainly don't want to fund research that would suggest we are! What about research into *treating* the fungal infections? That sounds like a far better idea."

"A treatment is certainly a great idea," said Leeman, "But due to high levels of resistance to existing antifungals, new developments tend to be in areas of immunology, which is not my specialism. I'd like to investigate the cause of the outbreak and take it from there."

"I'm a Doctor," said another board member. "We all know that healthy bacteria repopulates the mucous membranes very quickly following a course of antibiotics. The idea that fungi can cause anything more than a superficial infection in patients with fully functioning immune systems is ludicrous. And those infections are easy to treat."

"There are a growing number of infections that are not easy to treat," said Leeman.

"Fungal infections are a side effect of many medications," said the Doctor, "but that doesn't make us responsible for this outbreak." The others jeered in support.

"Absolutely!" said another suit, sternly. "Fungal infections are not new. Anything more than a superficial infection, is down to a serious secondary complication, like cancer treatment, HIV, or anti-rejection drugs for organ transplants. Our new drugs are not at fault. This theory is nonsense."

"I'm not saying we're responsible," said Leeman. "Just that there are a number of factors, including the recreational use of *Hot Caffeine*, which might have contributed to the rise in cases."

But they weren't listening. The others jeered in agreement with their colleagues and Leeman knew he'd just heard the prevailing view of the whole medical profession. Most of the fungal infections in this growing epidemic were superficial and being treated with antifungal drugs, so perhaps he was over-thinking this.

"I think I've just alienated the entire Board," Leeman said as he returned home to Jenny that evening.

"Oh. It didn't go well then?"

"Suffice to say, my request for funding was not granted. They're in denial."

"Oh dear. What did they say?"

"They're not interested in research that might be bad for business. And it seems the idea that pathogenic fungi could cause a serious problem among otherwise healthy individuals is unthinkable."

"Oh..."

"I just worry that antifungal treatments don't work for everyone, and there's a real risk of widespread resistance."

*   *   *

As time passed, it became clear that many of these superficial fungal infections were unresponsive to antifungal drugs, and the problem was spreading. New symptoms were emerging.

"Clinicians are saying that the fungal roots are burrowing deeper," Leeman said to his lab assistant, Pete Ward. "The infections are spreading and becoming chronic. I'm worried about an emerging epidemic. Traditional treatments seem to be completely ineffective for some people."

"My cousin's affected by it," replied Ward. "She tried our Smooth cream as a topical treatment, and it made it worse."

"Exactly. This also bothers me."

"Now she's feeling tipsy half the time. Puts it down to the infection. Weird."

"It *is* weird, but it's well documented. The feeling of inebriation is caused by fungal overgrowth in the gut, leading to fermentation of sugars. It's like the effect of brewers' yeast on malted barley to make beer. Fungi and yeasts are closely related. In the presence of fungi or yeasts, sugars turn to alcohol, which is released into people's bloodstreams, even when they haven't been drinking. And yes, it makes people feel tipsy."

"That's kinda crazy isn't it really!"

"It's not a good state of affairs when it's spreading across the population. Does your cousin take immuno-suppressive drugs or have any other issues with her immune system?"

"I don't think so."

"I am hearing that a lot of people with no previous history of immune suppression are experiencing untreatable symptoms. What a nightmare."

"Or an opportunity for us to deliver a cure?"

"Well I guess that's true, but we have nothing in the pipeline. It's not my area of expertise."

The scale of the problem was starting to challenge the widely-held belief that you can't get a serious fungal infection unless you first have a major failure of the immune system or immunosuppressive drugs.

A medical conference in London got onto the topic during a staged Q&A. "The idea that we have an epidemic of untreatable fungal infections is simply nonsense!" said a senior doctor on the stage. "It's just balderdash! Most of the people with so-called fungal infections have failed to demonstrate any sign of an actual infection. They have symptoms that can be attributed to other things. Or they've been diagnosed with a mild fungal infection at best. Their culture tests often come back negative, but GPs who don't know what else to do, offer treatment for fungal infections anyway, 'just in case'. Then they wonder why the treatment doesn't work.

"It doesn't work because it's not a fungal infection. A bit of keratin overgrowth is completely normal. Sores come and go. These things are nothing to worry about. They're not signs of a fungal infection. Moisturize and learn to live with it. This is not an epidemic of fungal infections. It's an epidemic of misdiagnosis by doctors who are over-stretched and don't have the tools or the expertise to make a proper diagnosis!"

The outburst caused a stir in the audience, and while not all the medics in the Q&A were quite so unsympathetic, there was a consensus that perhaps initial diagnoses had been wrong in a good number of cases. Positive results too, were often dismissed as 'contamination' - not evidence of an actual infection, especially when treatments failed to work.

"The numbers have been wildly inflated by well-meaning physicians, trying to help," said another expert, "and this has been perpetuated by the 'alternative medicine' fraternity, who put people on unhealthy diets, trying to 'starve the fungus' to death. It's not a healthy way of carrying on, and it's frankly no wonder that people are seeing secondary problems emerging while they're messing around with fad diets!"

There was much laughter and ridicule in the room. Meanwhile, people who insisted that their superficial fungal infections had spread were labeled as hypochondriacs.

The whole idea that healthy people could get serious fungal infections was too unconventional. It challenged everything that medics thought they knew, and bordered on agreement with the natural health lobby, who were a bunch of loonies.

But as healthy people around the world started going down with all the signs of chronic fungal infections, Leeman was

59

troubled. *Could these miracle drugs actually cause an epidemic of something worse?* He wanted to help.

Chapter 15
Smooth

Little Jessica was growing up fast. In a year's time she'd be off to secondary school, so she was really starting to take her school work seriously. Chewing *hot caffeine* had become a habit, but she and her friends obeyed the rules and didn't chew it at school. Her oral thrush had disappeared, but kept coming back – so it was just as well that the treatment was sweeties. Cool.

Then her skin started to go bad.

"Urgh! I've got spots!" Jessica was experiencing the joys of adolescence.

"Oh don't worry – everyone gets them at your age," said mum, Eve.

Jessica was mortified.

"You can get creams to make them go down you know," Eve tried to sound encouraging. "Can your friends recommend anything?"

Jessica pouted and phoned her friend Kate.

"My mum swears by a cream called 'Smooth' for anything!" said Kate, "It's supposed to kill infections and soften your skin."

Jessica told mum.

"Well, I guess we can try some, if that's what you want," said Eve, and the next day, she bought some while she was out. "Here you go," she gave the small tube to Jessica after school. Jessica smiled and ran to her room to try it out.

Within a couple of days her spots had visibly improved. "Mum! This is great stuff!" she yelled.

*   *   *

A regular visitor to the derelict, asbestos-riddled tower-block that Mark and Kevin called home, was Stephen, an unusual lad with a penchant for wearing women's clothes.

"What are you wearing, you silly sod?" Mark said in jest when Stephen came round donning a figure-hugging red frock one evening. Stephen smiled. Their mickey-taking was all in good humour. Mark flicked on the Ipod speakers to the familiar tune of *Dude looks like a Lady* by Aerosmith, and the threesome collapsed on the couch with beers.

"I'm having trouble with my makeup," Stephen complained. "The eye shadow's making my face go red and puffy."

"So stop wearing it!" Mark giggled.

"That's what the doctor said!" he complained. "But I don't feel properly dressed without it. I've been using the same brand for years and never had any trouble before."

This was very unsatisfactory. With make up, Stephen was a convincing woman. Without it, he was definitely a man in drag.

The threesome enjoyed clubbing at a seedy venue in London. It attracted all sorts of misfits – junkies, punks, transsexuals, prostitutes and their pimps. They all accepted one another, while many people in society treated them with disdain. It was a colourful scene of transvestite glamour, Mohican glory, raw bondage, and rough living. The dance floor displayed more energy than all the other East End clubs put together. This was where Stephen felt most at home - unjudged and accepted. He could just be himself.

The weekend arrived and the threesome headed into the capital - a funny looking trio, with two scruffs in denim, and Stephen dressed up to the nines. They walked through the darkened halls of the club, where Stephen's sequined dress caught the lights, and his shimmering white stockings glowed ultraviolet under the purple illuminations. Stilettos, a pink feather boa, a brown curly wig, and a pearl necklace with matching earrings completed the look.

"Don't you look gorgeous!" said a trans man in passing, Stephen grinned and returned the compliment. Make up was, of course, essential. He exchanged pleasantries with friends before heading for the dance floor with Kev, while Mark chilled on the sofa. When Stephen sat down, he spotted a petite blonde girl. "Ooh she's pretty!" he exclaimed.

"She's a junkie and she likes the macho type," said Kev. Stephen looked down at his frock and sighed. The bell for last orders rang and Stephen spotted a former lover, Barry, in the crowd, and went to speak to him.

"What's happened to your eyes? They're puffy!" exclaimed Barry. He looked disgusted, "It's letting your whole appearance down." The comment hurt. Stephen turned away, grief-stricken, and at a loss for words. Barry didn't seem interested in pursuing a relationship - or even in being friendly. Pity. The remarks concluded the evening on a sour note and the threesome caught the train home.

I need to sort this out, Stephen thought as he fell into a troubled sleep. As dawn came, he decided to leave his ladies' dresses in the wardrobe and abandon his makeup until this problem was resolved.

It was weeks later when Mark recommended a revolutionary new cream, called 'Smooth'. "It's really cool – it worked wonders on my sister's skin problems!" he enthused, and handed Stephen a tube. The young man applied the cream to his swollen eyelids, before bed. By morning there were signs of improvement.

He called the lads. "Hey Mark, this stuff's good!" he said.

Chapter 16
The Attack

David Leeman had become a sought-after speaker at universities, colleges, and corporate functions. He was enjoying life as a minor celebrity. Millions of people around the world admired his work, not least those whose lives had been changed for the better. Life was good. He and his wife, Jenny, moved into a luxurious Victorian house in West London.

One dark night, Leeman went outdoors to put the rubbish in the bin for the morning collection and he was approached by a scruffy man with a deranged look in his eyes.

"David Leeman right?"

"Erm, no. You're mistaken," said the scientist, sensing that this wasn't a friendly introduction.

"You're him all right. The so-called 'genius' who murders innocent animals." His breath stank of booze. It was Alex. "You brainwashed my girlfriend! You monster!"

Leeman shook his head, "No, you've got the wrong guy." He trod carefully as he edged back up the drive, towards his home.

Alex blocked his path.

"Look - I just help people," Leeman protested, edging away from his angry pursuer.

Alex lurched at the scientist, but in his tanked-up state, he missed. Leeman was able to dodge the drunkard, and escape into the safety of his house. He slammed the door shut. Alex picked himself up and thundered at the door with thumps and kicks. Leeman called the police and waited nervously, ushering Jenny to stay well away.

All went quiet. Then an axe came crashing through the front door. The couple hid upstairs, as the sound of splitting wood filled the air and the front door started to break down.

At that moment sirens sounded and two police cars came speeding down the street. Alex didn't hang around to see them.

He made a hasty exit, clambering over the garden wall. He'd vanished before the police could catch up with him.

"We'll take this as evidence," said the police officers, carefully removing the axe, which was still embedded in the broken door. They placed it carefully in a plastic bag. "We'll check it for fingerprints. You'll need to get this door boarded up until it can be replaced, and we'll get a couple of officers to watch the house for the next few nights. Can we come in? We'll need to write a full report."

"Yes, of course," said Leeman, inviting them in.

"Did you know the attacker?" asked one of the police officers.

"No. He knew who I was, but I didn't recognise him." Leeman shook his head. "It was weird and scary. He said I'd brainwashed his girlfriend, and I honestly don't know what he's talking about. I haven't brain washed anyone. Didn't sound like he's a fan of my work though. He said I murder innocent animals. I work in medical research. Perhaps an animal rights protestor?"

"Possibly. Can you give us a description of his appearance?"

"I'd say he was in his 30s, dark hair, just short of six foot. He was full of rage and covered in wounds and bandages."

"OK. That's interesting. Do you have any CCTV outside?"

"No, but there's a council camera just up the road, which might have caught him."

"OK we'll check that out."

They chatted a while longer, then the police left, while Leeman boarded up the door.

"Good job you had a board in the shed," said Jenny.

"I thought it might come in useful one day. Don't like to get rid of anything that might be useful!"

"I hope he doesn't come back."

"Me too. Nasty piece of work. No idea what he was on about."

The couple slept a little less comfortably in their beds that night. Perhaps this media circus around Leeman's medical breakthrough wasn't such a good thing after all.

Late the following day, there was an unexpected knock at the side door. They ignored it. Then another knock, louder and harsher than the first. "I'll get a knife!" Jenny whispered. She scampered into the kitchen before he could argue and returned with a large kitchen knife. Leeman took it from her and slowly approached the door.

"Mr and Mrs Leeman - it's the police," a voice echoed through the locked door. Leeman sighed with relief and opened the door to see a large uniformed policeman standing outside.

"I'm sorry if I alarmed you by coming to the side door. After all the damage to the front door, I thought it might be better to use this one! We've matched the fingerprints we took yesterday to an escapee from a psychiatric hospital. He has a particular hatred of the life sciences industry and has been imprisoned for offences related to animal testing and violent protests before. We have people out looking for him in the local area. We're keeping an eye on his previous addresses and old friends, and we're still keeping an eye on your house. If anything unsettling happens we're right outside."

"Thank you. That's good to know." Leeman nodded and thanked him. The couple busied themselves with household chores for the next few hours, then Jenny went upstairs to prepare for bed. As she emerged from the bathroom, she heard a sound from the bedroom.

"Are you in bed already?" she asked jovially, and pushed the door open. Alex darted towards her, pounced, knocking her to the floor, and held her down. She screamed, but her cries were quickly cut short as a razor-sharp knife sliced into her throat, and blood soaked the carpet.

Leeman was already flying up the stairs, two at a time, by it was too late for Jenny. The police, who had heard the disturbance from outside, burst through the door. Alex appeared at the top of the stairs. A shot rang out and Alex fell to the ground, injured, with a bloody arm.

Jenny lay lifeless on the bedroom floor. Leeman wept, full of grief, pain, and anger. Would these animal rights activists stop at nothing for their cause?

*   *   *

The following morning Terry flicked on the TV, "Jenny Leeman, the wife of Nobel Prize winner David Leeman, was murdered last night in her West London home. The murder was seemingly without motive. A man in his 30s, reported to be mentally unstable, broke into the family home at 10.30pm. He was arrested at the scene, but it was too late for Mrs Leeman who disturbed the intruder."

"Oh no!" cried Terry. She was a huge fan of David Leeman and his work.

*   *   *

Jessica had begun to notice some small white speckles on her face. They were pale, and had been there for a few months. At first she wondered if it was her acne coming back, but this was different. 'Smooth' had cleared the acne, pretty much permanently. *Perhaps it's just the winter chill,* she thought. *They're not very noticeable; not like zits. They'll probably disappear when it warms up a bit. Probably nothing to worry about.* But as more weeks passed and they didn't go away, she started to wonder.

"Have you noticed anything funny about my face mum?" she asked one day.

"No. Why?" asked Eve.

"I've got tiny white spots," She tried to point to some.

"Oh that – I thought it was just the weather. Does it bother you?"

"A bit. They've been there for ages!"

"Have you tried moisturising?"

"Yes - and I used Smooth. Neither made any difference."

She decided to see her doctor about it. "I'm afraid I have no idea what it is," he admitted, "perhaps a reaction to the winter chill? Try wrapping up more carefully, and covering your lower face with a scarf when you're out in the cold winds. If it doesn't go away in a month or two, then do come back and I'll refer you to a dermatologist."

She left the surgery disappointed and covered up more thoroughly for the next few weeks. It didn't help. She decided to persevere using 'Smooth' on her skin, to see if it cleared the speckles - after all, it had done wonders for her acne. At first it made no difference, but in time, the milky spots got worse. Smooth definitely wasn't helping this time. She put the tube away in a drawer.

"I'm starting to look ugly and blotchy!" she complained to mum. Tears rolled down her face. She felt embarrassed. "People will think I'm ugly!"

"Oh sweetheart! It's not that bad. You could never be ugly."

Jessica stood there sobbing.

"You're beautiful," insisted Eve. "The speckles aren't that noticeable. We'll go back to the doctor and see what he can do. Try not to worry. I'll get you some makeup and we can cover them up. No one will notice. I promise." That was reassuring, but Jessica was feeling anxious. She dried her tears and tried to think positive.

Back at the surgery, six weeks after the initial visit, the doctor looked surprised at the worsening of her condition.

"Oh dear — I'll make you an emergency appointment with a dermatologist. We can't have this can we!" He was kind and she was reassured by his words.

Weeks passed, and Jessica wore makeup to hide the blemishes. Eventually she received a letter from the dermatologist's office, telling her that an appointment had been made with the dermatologist, in two months' time.

"So much for an emergency appointment!" said Eve. She phoned to see if an earlier appointment was available, but that was the earliest date, barring a cancellation. This was going to be a difficult time.

Kids at school noticed that Jessica had started wearing makeup and initially thought she was just experimenting. Then a group of high-spirited girls splashed her face in the showers after PE, and the water revealed subtle blemishes. Soon they were teasing her about it and calling her names. "Zombie! Blotch face!" they'd laugh. They burst into hysterics as tears welled up in her eyes.

Chapter 17
Prison

Arrested at the scene of Jenny Leeman's murder, Alex was banged up awaiting trial. This was a tough prison regime, not a cushy hospital with caring nurses and drugs to take the edge off his festering anger and resentment. At lunchtime the prisoners filed out of their cells towards the canteen. A few harsh words were exchanged en route and a punch was thrown by a short tough guy who was immediately restrained and dragged back to his cell by two prison officers.

"You've got no right to stop me from having some food!" he bellowed as they dragged him away.

Lunch was served – mashed potato, greens, and a slab of tofu - the vegan choice, not very appetising, but at least they respected his vegan lifestyle. Alex picked up a knife and fork and sat alone at the end of the table. He didn't want any trouble and he planned to keep himself to himself.

Over the next few weeks, he kept his head down and attended one-to-one sessions with a prison psychiatrist, "Tell me Alex," she said, "How did your activism come to this?"

"I was driven to it," he replied, "My partner, Terry, took part in a clinical trial with one of the pharmaceutical companies. It was a selfish decision. We'd both been fighting against the torture of animals in medicine for decades, but she switched sides – just like that! Brainwashed by them she was!"

"And Terry? Where is she now?"

"We split up. I couldn't handle it. Then she testified against me..."

In the sessions that ensued, they discussed his background, the arson attack, and his motivations and beliefs. After a series of therapy sessions leading to an assessment, the psychiatrist reported that Alex had Borderline Personality Disorder. The psychiatric institution from which he'd escaped was more interested in keeping the peace and sedating patients, than in providing diagnoses, offering therapy, or uncovering the reasons behind their patients' anger management issues. The diagnosis might provide a helpful basis for future therapy, but it wasn't going to get him out of jail.

"OK, We're going to trial next week," said his barrister. "You're charged with the murder of Jenny Leeman, GBH against your old psychiatric nurse, and you still have time to serve for arson.

"Under the circumstances I'd recommend you plead not guilty on the grounds of diminished responsibility.

"Again? I hated that institution."

"Yes, well you need to stop hurting people if you want to stay out of institutions. You were caught fleeing the scene of a murder and there's compelling evidence against you. You're unlikely to get off if you plead not guilty. Diminished responsibility kept you out of jail last time, and now you have a formal diagnosis of BPD, which could help your case. I can't see we have any other choice. If your plea is accepted, you'd go down for manslaughter, which means you might get out one day. If you go down for murder, you'll probably be incarcerated for life.

"I can also suggest that you're better suited to a hospital environment than a prison... I truly believe that. I think in a regular prison, the other inmates will wind you up and exacerbate your anger issues."

"That's true. I'm keeping my head down at the moment, but I've done time before and that's exactly what happens," Alex confessed.

"I'm guessing you come out more angry than you went in?"

"Yes, I do."

"So do you agree? Do you want to plead diminished responsibility?"

Despite his dislike of psychiatric hospitals, Alex had to admit he was in a tight spot. Hospital readmission seemed like a better option than serving a life sentence in a prison cell. Either way, the situation was depressing.

"The defendant has unresolved childhood traumas and severe Borderline Personality Disorder," said the prison psychiatrist. "He needs help, not punishment."

The hospital psychiatrist from his previous institution had a less forgiving view. "This man has a dangerous, extremist belief system and has shown little sign of remorse, except for the fact that he was caught. He's a danger to society and he needs to be kept under lock and key in a secure psychiatric institution with the correct facilities to address his anger, challenge his beliefs, and support his rehabilitation. He should not be set free for a very long time."

The prosecuting barrister felt differently and pulled no punches. "I put it to the court that this man is guilty of premeditated murder and deserves to be sent to prison for life," he said. "I'm going to present evidence to prove it."

He called David Leeman to the stand and asked him to describe the events that took place the night before his wife's death. The scientist broke down in tears, giving his testimony and explaining how it all ended. The police officers present at the scene gave their testimonies too.

Over the next week, the evidence was laid out before the jury: eye witnesses in the neighbourhood, DNA, the circumstances in which Alex was found immediately after the killing, with blood-strained hands and the weapon, a large knife, covered with his fingerprints. It was an open and shut case. Adding a few years for GBH when he knocked out the psychiatric nurse, was more of a formality.

What wasn't so straight forward, however, was whether to treat him as a patient or a prisoner. With two psychiatric assessments stating he needed psychiatric care, the judge sentenced him to indefinite confinement in Newfield Psychiatric Hospital – a secure institution, that would perhaps be his home for the rest of his life.

Chapter 18
Terry

Terry had begun to notice speckles appearing on her body. They didn't hurt so she didn't worry about it, but when they started to get bigger, she checked with her doctor.

"I don't think it's anything to worry about," he said. "It will probably go away in its own time, but if it persists, do feel free to come back and see me."

She left, happy to monitor the situation, but within a few months, her skin was quite discoloured in places - a creamy colour. She returned to the surgery.

"It started out as little speckles, but it's getting worse," she complained. "In the worst areas, it's sore and itchy."

"You've had a lot of success with Smooth in the past haven't you?" he said.

"Yes, but this is different. The Smooth cream doesn't help. I tried."

"OK. Let me take a look," he said. She pulled her sleeve up. "Ahh, I see. Well, it could be Vitiligo, a loss of pigment in the skin, but that doesn't seem quite right. Vitiligo wouldn't make your skin sore, just discoloured. There are camouflage creams that can be applied to restore some colour to affected areas, but let's try some hydrocortisone cream first. It reduces inflammation, so it should help with the itching and soreness. It might sort out the discolouration too, but if it doesn't help, come back and I'll refer you to a dermatologist." He wrote a prescription and sent Terry on her way.

The hydrocortisone cream was useless, so she reported back to the doctor a few weeks later, and while she waited for a referral to see a dermatologist, she bought a new tube of 'Smooth'.

This stuff helped me so much in the past, I wonder if I haven't given it enough of a chance. She lavishly applied it to her skin.

Overnight, her condition worsened. *Oh no! This is awful!* Worried that her old complaint might be making a resurgence, she liberally applied more Smooth that night, trying to achieve a better result.

Again, her condition worsened, and when she returned to the pharmacy to buy more 'Smooth', the assistant said, "Are you sure it's not this cream that's making your problem worse?"

She hadn't thought of that – she'd been so blinkered by its miraculous results in the past, it hadn't crossed her mind that for this particular condition, it might make things worse. By the time she returned to see her doctor again, she looked quite ill. Parts of her skin were pale, blotchy and itchy. The receptionist kept her distance, looked concerned, and shooed her towards the waiting area.

Terry was called into the Doctor's office. He looked up at her and his face turned pale. "I... I... don't understand!" he stuttered.

"Neither do I," came Terry's brief reply.

"How has this got so much worse since we last spoke?"

"I was hoping you'd tell me that."

The doctor pulled on some latex gloves, stood up, moved towards Terry, and probed her face in disbelief, "Is your whole body like this?"

"Yes."

"The hydrocortisone cream obviously didn't help."

"No."

He tapped into his PC, "Ah yes, you've had skin complaints before haven't you. The new 'Smooth' cream cleared them up. Is that right?"

"Yes but it wasn't like this. I had nasty rashes that came and went, but they were different - red and painful. They looked completely different. Besides, I tried Smooth again, because the hydrocortisone cream didn't do anything."

"It didn't help this time?"

"No. I think it might have made it worse. I had blind faith in Smooth, so was applying it liberally until the pharmacist suggested that it might be making my condition worse."

"Oh dear. Well that's possible. Maybe an allergic reaction." He paused for thought. "Did you ever get a fungal infection while using it before?"

"Yes, but I treated it, and it went away eventually."

"I wonder if that's the root of this problem." He looked concerned. "I'll do some tests and chase up the dermatologist for an emergency appointment. I can only prescribe pain killers, but you need specialist help. I'd suggest you moisturise if you think that's helpful."

He paused and rummaged around in his drawer, before passing over a pamphlet. "This is a new NHS pamphlet about dermatology and different skin conditions - do have a read and if you think any of the conditions relate to your experiences, discuss it with the dermatologist when you get an appointment. I'll take a swab and run a test for a fungal infection. Chin up. We'll get to the bottom of this."

Terry left the surgery feeling depressed. An emergency appointment came through by the end of the week - they could see her in two weeks' time. Just as well really, as the test for a fungal infection was negative and her GP didn't know what to do.

Chapter 19
Jessica

The dermatologist sat Jessica and Eve down, "Can you tell me how this all began?"

Jessica looked blankly at her, "I don't know. I mean, the white spots just appeared out of nowhere. I wasn't too bothered at first because they were faint and difficult to see, but then they got bigger, and whiter, and now they're horrible and starting to itch!"

"Have you been using any treatments on your face?"

"Only the anti-acne cream, 'Smooth'."

"And what happened?"

"It seemed to make the white spots worse."

"Then don't use it," she advised. "Your problem could be caused by an allergy or sensitivity to cosmetics, wipes, or a cream you've been using."

"I wasn't using anything on my skin when it started," she looked perplexed.

"It could be a food allergy or a reaction to some kind of soap or detergent," she suggested. "Can you keep a diary of all the foods you eat and the soaps and shampoos you wash with, and we'll meet again to see if we can spot any patterns emerging? In the meantime, try some dermatological cream," She wrote out a prescription. "This might help. I'd also like a nurse to take some blood before you leave – it might help us pick up any abnormalities."

The test results came back normal, which didn't help. The food and chemicals diary didn't seem to tally anything specific with flare ups. The dermatological cream didn't really seem to do anything either. Jessica felt humiliated and was starting to lose faith in medicine.

"There's one other possibility," said the dermatologist. Jessica looked hopeful.

"If the mild antibiotic in 'Smooth' made it worse, then it could be that it's a fungus."

"A fungus?"

"It's unlikely – but not impossible. Healthy individuals don't usually get fungal infections, apart from superficial ones on their feet and nails, but if the circumstances are such that your immune system has been compromised, it's possible that this could be caused by a fungus. I'll do a test."

More weeks passed. The test was negative, and Jessica's hopes started to slip away.

"I'm going to refer you to another specialist," said the dermatologist.

"More specialist that you?" she asked.

"Yes, he's an expert in a rare skin condition called vitiligo. I think that might be what you've got, but I'd like his expert opinion."

"What can be done if that's the problem?" she asked.

"One step at a time," she didn't seem to want to commit.

Back at home, Jessica Googled vitiligo and quickly discovered that the cause was unknown and there was no cure. It could be exacerbated by worry. *It's hard not to worry!* she thought.

Within a few weeks, she received her appointment with the consultant, Mr Patel.

He took a good look at her and sighed. "This is not vitiligo." He had a strong Asian accent. "To me, it looks like some kind of parasitic infection… perhaps a fungus."

"But my tests for a fungal infection came back negative."

"Oh and so often they do, but the drugs work anyway!" he said jovially.

"Let me try you on a low dose of Fluconazole for two weeks and then I'd like you to come back and we'll see if it's any better."

The drug didn't touch it. The white spots started to become slightly raised on her skin.

"If it's not fungal," he said, "I'm confident it's just keratin overgrowth – your own skin forming an abnormal top layer. It's not harmful, but it can be irritating and unsightly. I'll give you some cream to reduce the overgrowth, and you can use it as required," he said apologetically. "That's all we can do, but don't worry. Often it goes away on its own."

She returned home feeling confused. The medics didn't seem to know what was going on. What if it didn't go away?

Time passed, the bullies got bored and Jessica learnt to manage her condition, using the cream supplied by Mr Patel. She used makeup to improve skin tone. Some of her peers were slowly developing the same problem, so she was no longer singled out as a freak. It was becoming alarmingly normal, and while many medics dismissed the distress of young girls as 'vanity', many in society were becoming very uneasy about the escalation of unsightly skin conditions in the western world.

After a long period of the blues, poor sleep, and avoidance of social situations, Jessica finally seemed to move beyond a preoccupation with her appearance to develop an outward focus and a new lease of life. She started secondary school, and made new friends. She was cheerful, hard working - an inspiration. She went on a big spending spree to upgrade her wardrobe. She couldn't afford it, but Eve was just glad to see her happy and would straighten out Jessica's finances later.

Jessica however, started behaving really strangely – out of character. She caused a fuss in a restaurant about nothing, got really angry, and went from extremely high moods to extreme lows.

"I'm worried about you love," said Eve. "Why these mood swings? Are you taking something?"

"Only *hot caffeine,* for relaxation," she replied. Nothing new there then. Eve dropped her daughter at the youth club. "Do you want me to pick you up later?"

"I can walk back when it's over," thanks mum. Eve watched from a distance as she went inside. She recognised the crowd and the atmosphere was clearly jovial, until a lad walked up to Jessica and started speaking to her. *Who's that?* thought Eve. *He doesn't look friendly.* Everyone's faces dropped and it was clear, he was poking fun at Jessica's appearance. Onlookers frowned and Jessica's friend waved her arms aggressively, shooing him away.

The youth leader stepped in, grabbing the bully by the collar. He threw him out of the hall. As the bully tumbled down the steps into the cold night air he was hurling abuse.

Eve looked back, resisting the urge to go and rescue her daughter - Jessica was growing up fast and wouldn't want her mum fighting her battles...

The mood picked up and the girls seemed happy again. Eve drove home, content that Jess was in good company.

"Just hanging out with Sammy for a bit," Jessica texted later, so Eve didn't worry.

She got back home at 10.30pm, light headed and stinking of booze. "Jess! What have you been doing?"

"Hanging out with Sammy in the park."

"Drinking."

"A bit. Not a lot. She's got strawberry cider. Just thought I'd try some. Quite nice actually."

"Oh Jess, you need to be careful. You're still young, and vulnerable."

Jess shrugged. "I'm 12 years old! Stop hassling me!" She went to bed.

Jessica seemed to be changing and Eve didn't understand why. *Is it normal teenage rebellion, or something more? Her behaviour's so erratic these days – happy one minute and deeply depressed the next.* She was taking *hot caffeine* more often, to lift her mood on the bad days.

Over the next few weeks, Jess stayed out more, and would come home drunk and gobby some nights. Other nights, she was the perfect daughter, immaculately behaved.

Am I too soft? Eve wondered. *I don't like to be strict with her. She's basically a good kid. Sensible. I don't mind her experimenting, but some of this is so out of character.*

A lad came round that Jessica had had a crush on, Tommy. They made out on the sofa. Eve wasn't surprised she liked him, but snogging on the sofa? At 12?

Better than shenanigans in the bedroom, I suppose. Perhaps it's just part of growing up. Normal teenage rebellion.

They had a chat. "It's just kissing. I really like him mum!"

"OK. But don't let him pressure you. You're still a child. Keep your clothes on. Respect yourself and keep it simple."

"I'm not a slapper mum!"

"I don't think you are Jess. I just don't trust him."

"Honestly mum, I don't want him to see my body. It's fat, embarrassing, and my skin looks horrible under my clothes."

"Oh Jess, You're not fat. You're beautiful. I thought the cream Mr Patel gave you was helping your skin?"

"It rubs off on my clothes so it doesn't work as well there. So you see, I'm not going to sleep with him. Do you feel better now?"

"Perhaps it's time to follow up with the doctor."

"We've seen two specialists. I doubt there's any more they can do."

"Oh Jess, I'm so sorry."

A few weeks later, Jessica was acting odd. "I love you so much mum."

"I love you too! What's this all about then?"

"Oh nothing. Just saying... Tommy says my skin's gross. We split up."

"Tommy's a nasty little boy. Told you he was no good."

"Hmmm."

Jess headed upstairs to her room and slumped on the bed. *This skin disease is ruining my life. I hate myself. I'm ugly. I've got revolting skin. I feel awful. I'm moody and feeling shit most of the time.*

Tears rolled down her cheeks. *Nobody likes me and I'm totally depressed. My life is not worth living. I can't stand the sight of myself in the mirror. How can I expect anyone else to like me. No one will ever love me. My life is over.*

She sobbed into her pillow.

Eve heard her and knocked. "Can I come in?"

"Yes," Jess choked back the tears.

Eve sat on the bed and put her arm around Jess. "You'll be OK. Tommy was no good. You can do better."

"It's not just him. This disease is ruining my life. It's getting worse and worse."

"The doctor did say it might go away in time."

"Wishful thinking."

"Awww come here. Try to think positive." They had a big hug.

"I want to have a sleep," said Jess.

"OK. I'll leave you alone. Shout if you need anything."

Jess lay on her bed, staring at the ceiling. *My future is so bleak. I'm a total burden. Mum would be better off without me.*

She lay there for a while, negative thoughts rolling around in her head, then she reached for a vegetable knife that she'd been using to cut an apple earlier in the day. Firmly in her right hand, she slid the blade swiftly across her left wrist and watched the blood flow freely. She felt no real pain – it would all be over soon anyway. Nothing mattered any more. She did the same to her right wrist and blood poured from both wounds, staining the beige carpet. Jessica fell unconscious.

Eve came up 10 minutes later and knocked on the bedroom door, "Jessica?" She pushed the door open and saw her daughter in a pool of blood on the floor. Checking for a pulse, she found a weak heartbeat, then called an ambulance and wrapped Jessica's bleeding wrists in towels to stop the flow.

"I don't understand," she said to the paramedic on the way to the hospital. "I knew she'd been battling with difficult feelings about the way she looked, and her boyfriend just ended their relationship... but they'd only been seeing each other for a couple of weeks. I had no idea she was feeling this bad." She held her head in her hands. "She was a bit tearful earlier, but then she said she just wanted to sleep. I left her alone to get some shut eye. I thought she'd be OK."

"Don't beat yourself up. It's hard to predict it when things like this happen," he said. "You can't always tell. We've got her in time. She'll be OK."

In A&E, the doctors patched Jessica up and monitored her. When she regained consciousness, she was given some time with a psychiatrist and kept in for observation.

"I hate being here!" she complained to nurses, then ran off when no one was looking. She ran out of the building, passed Eve in the car park, and continued down the road, crying, "I'm going to the cemetery to die!" Eve ran after her.

"Stop!" she cried out. "You have to go back to hospital. You're not well." Eve grabbed Jessica's arm, forcing her to stop.

"Leave me alone! I just want it to be over! I want to die!" she screamed.

"I'll never leave you when you're like this," said mum, tears welling up in her eyes. Eve hugged her and Jessica burst into tears. They walked back to the hospital together, where Jessica was placed in a private room. Eve stayed with her and Jessica sat there looking terrified with her arms in bandages.

"I just want them to leave me alone," she said in a sad tone. She looked beaten.

Following a psychiatric assessment and some tests, the doctor asked Eve to join them. "Your daughter is showing signs of bipolar," he explained. "And her regular use of *hot caffeine* has probably made her symptoms worse."

"Oh dear. I wasn't very comfortable with the *hot caffeine*," said Eve, "but all her friends were using it, and you can't stop them when it's growing everywhere."

"It's not just that. Sometimes these things have a genetic basis too, or a predisposition."

"OK. Can you help her?"

"Yes, we have medications to regulate her emotions and stop her from experiencing such dramatic mood swings, from highs to lows and back again."

"I am here you know," interrupted Jessica.

"Yes love. Sorry. How do you feel about this?"

"Even more depressed, to be honest. Isn't bipolar just a polite word for manic depression."

"We don't use that term any more, but there are periods of depression and periods of extreme elation, yes. What we need to do, is to help you manage it, so you don't experience such extremes."

"Maybe I like the 'happy' episodes."

"You don't like the downs though do you," he looked at her wrists.

"Hmph," she turned away.

"When can she come home?" asked Eve.

"The bleeding's stopped, so she can go home when she's ready, as long as you feel able to look after her."

"OK. Would you like to come home, sweetheart?"

Jess nodded.

"All right, if you're sure," the doctor said.

"I think we're sure," Eve squeezed Jess's hand.

"Here's a prescription then," said the doctor, "but let's book a follow up session too. I can help you to manage bipolar with medication, and also to recognise the triggers for episodes of deep depression and episodes of mania, should they persist. You're not on your own here."

Eve thanked the doctor and took Jessica home.

Chapter 20
Epidemic

Stephen, the cross-dresser, went to see his doctor. Funny pale speckles had appeared around his eyes. 'Smooth' had previously resolved an unpleasant reaction to his makeup, so he tried it again - but this time it was different. This time, 'Smooth' seemed to make his problem worse.

The plump doctor lounged back in a large leather chair, "How can I help you son?" he smiled.

"I've got a problem with the skin around my eyes," he looked away embarrassed. He didn't think the doctor was taking him seriously.

The doctor stood up to get a closer look, inspecting Stephen's face intently. "Hmmm. I've seen this before," he said. "It's becoming quite a common problem I'm afraid. We don't know the cause – all we know is that it's increasingly prevalent, and that it can be quite distressing. At the moment, there is no cure. I have a leaflet about it, which tells you how the disease progresses and what to expect. It's not life-threatening, but it can zap your confidence."

Stephen looked dismayed. "So there's nothing you can do?"

"Well, " he paused for thought. "It's not all bad news. There's a lot of research going into it, so stay in touch if it doesn't go away by itself. There may be new treatments coming onto the market in due course. In the meantime, I'd suggest you just cover it with a concealer, and try not to worry. Stress can make lots of things worse, so try to relax, and just avoid anything that you think might be causing it."

Stephen left the surgery feeling depressed. Over the weeks that followed, the spots started to spread, discolouring his cheeks too. He was no stranger to makeup, but he was starting to feel embarrassed. There was a limit to what could be done with concealer! He made excuses to friends, feeling too self-conscious to go out. It was horrible.

* * *

New brands of heavy makeup, creams and concealers, all designed specifically to hide the growing emergence of patchy skin problems, became best-sellers as the number of people reporting the same symptoms - unsightly discolouration, pale spots and blemishes, soreness and dry skin, escalated.

Then people affected by these problems started reporting digestive complaints too, fatigue, and a host of other strange ailments, including brain fog and dizziness. Were they related? Were the secondary complaints caused by stress? No one knew. Blood tests and biopsies were coming back normal. It was like mass hysteria, but the physical evidence of disease could not be ignored.

BBC Television News: "People around the world are complaining of unsightly skin problems, which until now, have been dismissed by doctors as cosmetic and not serious. But they're becoming so common that surgeries and clinics are struggling with the numbers of people asking for help. Doctor Portman explains, 'The symptoms are not life threatening, but we appreciate that it's causing people some distress. There is a view that the condition is stress-related and if people just try to relax it will pass and clear up on it's own. However, it's early days and there is research underway. We're asking people to be patient. Sometimes moisturising can help, and there is a cream on the market that helps remove dead skin cells - this might alleviate some of the symptoms."

The camera switched to a busy clinic. "Look! How can anyone say this is normal?" said a woman with whitish discolouration on her face. "It's horrible! I'm a freak!"

An epidemic was unfolding, and while it wasn't thought to be contagious, there were a lot of unknowns. The research left more questions than answers. Was it an allergic reaction to something? Was it an infection? Bacteria? Fungi? Parasitic? Something in the water? Pollution? Something else? As best they could tell, it was just an abnormal response of the skin, but to what? *That* was a mystery. No one knew what was causing it. They still didn't understand how it spread or how it could be contained – and it seemed virtually impossible to cure. It was very distressing for all those afflicted, and caused much misery.

Conspiracy theorists were convinced there was something darker going on - a government cover up.

Chapter 21
Research

After Jenny's death, David Leeman lost interest in his career and opted out of medical research to follow a simpler life. He'd made his mark as the genius scientist who developed life-changing medicines. But everything about the past reminded him of his loss, so he stepped back and chose to live quietly, away from the public eye.

His former colleagues at Cother Pharmaceuticals however, were still working on cutting-edge research and new product development. Engaged with a team of international scientists, one of his former colleagues, Jonathan Melluish, was immersed in studying the epidemic of skin disease that had spread across the world. Could they draw conclusive results, or find a cure, where all those before had failed? It was a hell of a challenge.

There are so many questions and so few answers, he thought. *What's the underlying cause? Why are increasing numbers of people experiencing other symptoms such as digestive complaints, extreme tiredness and dizziness?*

"I'm of the view that we're looking at two different complaints," he said in a team meeting. "The fact that they're often seen together is perhaps an indication that the immune system is under pressure. But the digestive difficulties and exhaustion look to me like they're independent of the skin complaints. I think we need different approaches to treatment for the different symptoms."

"Or a single drug that boosts people's immunity naturally," suggested his colleague. "There's some great work going on in immunology."

"True, but so far, drugs designed to boost immunity have been ineffective against this disease. At the moment, it's all about managing symptoms. If we can help people manage their symptoms more effectively, that's progress."

* * *

Terry flicked on the TV just in time to catch the breaking news: "We're outside the Houses of Parliament, where today the British government has declared a state of emergency. Protestors outside are calling for more action to end the epidemic of disease, which is starting to spread around the world. Here in the UK, hospitals and doctors' surgeries are overwhelmed with people demanding to be seen. People are experiencing new symptoms and going off sick from work, with more people reporting symptoms with every passing day."

The camera zoomed in on protestors chanting, "Stop the disease!"

"I'm a nurse and we're seeing this epidemic spreading like wildfire," said Jack.

"What are you seeing on the frontline?" asked the reporter.

"The disease has become more aggressive," he shouted over the noise. "Symptoms are appearing earlier and spreading more quickly. Treatments seem less effective than they were. People with diseased skin are increasingly reporting dizziness and a feeling of drunkenness. Many people are complaining that the treatments are no good. They used to help, but not so much now. I gotta go, or I might get into trouble!"

"Thank you Jack," said the reporter as he rushed off. There was a kafuffle nearby. "The Health Secretary is coming to speak to us." He stepped into view. "What's the latest news, sir?"

The Health Secretary said, "We don't think the disease is contagious in the early stages, but there's mounting speculation that it may become contagious as it develops. Some people seem to recover quickly and fight it off, so we mustn't over-react. However, to stop the spread, in densely populated areas, people who are seriously ill will be placed under quarantine. You'll start to see military interventions in areas badly affected by the outbreak. People are advised to comply with military instructions. This is not a voluntary measure. There's no cause for alarm as they'll get the very best treatment in these facilities."

"What does that mean for my mum?" screamed a protestor. He ignored her.

"We're asking the pharmaceutical companies to work together to find treatments," he continued. "We have allocated £2 billion to speed up this process. There are clinical trials already in progress, so the outlook is promising. But the best thing people can do, is avoid crowded places and carry on with their lives. These protests are not helping. They are simply adding to our problems. Please go home." The Health Secretary went back inside as angry people screamed and shouted at him.

The reporter went to speak to a woman who'd been screaming - she was being held back by police. "Do you want to tell us your story?"

"Yes! I don't understand what's happening to my mum. Her skin's horrible. She's so exhausted, she just can't function properly. I'm really concerned. The doctors are at a loss and the medicines don't seem to help any more. Now they're saying they'll take her into quarantine. This is terrifying!"

"It really is," said the reporter, sympathetically. She turned to the camera, "The good news is that researchers are working around the clock to find treatments. One fascinating observation that scientists are exploring, is that less developed countries are much less affected by the outbreak. They're looking at these regions in search of answers. It might be that the disease is somehow related to our modern lifestyles in the west.

"While experts work tirelessly to find new treatments, some prescription medicines that may offer relief will be available over the counter from next week. This will enable people with mild symptoms to access treatments without a doctor's appointment."

* * *

Patients were entering hospitals with increasingly nasty infections - superficial discolouration, lesions, and severe inflammation. Those in constant contact with them - medical staff and families - became infected too, and shortages of protective equipment became a growing problem and a source of much criticism in the media.

Patients were given pain killers, anti-inflammatory drugs, and sedatives as a sense of weary, tearful, panic set in. Following treatment, some returned home with medical supplies and clear instructions on how to manage their condition.

Researchers around the world were working to find a treatment or cure, but were no closer to identifying the underlying cause. They started clinical trials, testing different creams, anti-inflammatory drugs, and new anti-microbial drugs - some appeared to offer modest benefits.

As promised, specialist facilities were set up on the outskirts of cities, with the military taking those seriously affected by the disease from the hospitals to emergency units set up to treat the most sick. Some of those in the new facilities were given the chance to take part in new drug trials.

This freed up the hospitals to treat those with less severe symptoms and continue their routine operations, but this provided no comfort for frightened relatives. "There's no visitor access and no information!" complained one tearful woman, who'd been hoping to visit her sister.

Military personnel intervened where hospices had been caring for those with life-threatening conditions, exacerbated by underlying disease. They took patients from the hospices to the specialist units for ongoing treatment, to contain the spread. Inside, people were sedated and kept comfortable, but there was only so much they could do until better treatments were found.

Outside in the wider world, people tried all sorts of creams to treat mild conditions - Smooth, dermatological creams, natural butters, and many branded products, but few offered any benefit and some made it worse. By the time it became common knowledge that anti-inflammatories might be helpful, they were mostly sold out, with retailers experiencing supply problems. It was becoming clear that the medical profession didn't understand this disease at all.

The intake of *hot caffeine* was at an all time high, because people needed escapism and a way to relax, but the highs of the drug did little to offset the real-life disaster unfolding around them.

Chapter 22
Time for Change

The British Prime Minister banged on the Cabinet Room table in frustration. He needed more from his advisors, "This is really serious!" he said. "I'm frustrated by the lack of progress. Our workforces are getting ill, our economy's at risk, families are being split up. We have the best researchers in the world working together on this. Yet they've been unable to find a solution. We need to step up our response, fast!"

"There is one man Sir," said one of his advisors.

"Yes?"

"David Leeman – he was the brains behind the revolutionary new antibiotics. He's considered to be among the world's best minds in medical research but he's been in mourning ever since his wife was murdered. He withdrew from society and opted out of pharmaceuticals, which is why he's not on the research team." The others nodded, agreeing. "We can contact him. He's been known to succeed where others have failed before. He made himself unpopular with some controversial ideas years ago, but he might be our best hope - if he'll step up and take on the challenge."

"Yes, please contact him! We need everyone working on this. I mean *everyone* who shows potential. Bring out the best retired folk and the best students. We need brilliant minds wherever they are."

*   *   *

When Leeman received the call, in a sense, he was relieved. He'd been in mourning for a long time. Perhaps this new focus would be good for him - a new challenge and a reason to move on.

As part of the familiarity process with the project, he met a number of patients suffering from the disease. One such patient was Jessica, a special young teenager, who was now struggling with yellowing patches sporadically growing over her body. She wasn't bad enough to be confined in camps, but she did worry about passing it on, and had less social contact these days. The disease had zapped her confidence and made her feel bad, so a degree of social-isolation came naturally.

"How are you Jessica?" he asked.

"I just want to get better so I can see my friends again."

"Quite right too. Let's see if we can get you back to full health. It might take some time, but bear with us. I'll do my very best." His encouraging remarks offered a glimmer of hope as he examined the growths on her skin.

Back at the government research laboratory, he was discussing the project with the team. "Before taking a break, I was studying DNA sequencing of disease-causing organisms," he explained, "and I was on track to develop a new technology, that overcomes many of the challenges, complexities and limitations of existing approaches.

"Why haven't we tried it before?" asked his colleague.

"It was part of a top-secret project that got dropped when the money ran out. We didn't want competitors getting wind of the technology. But with funding, I can pick up where we left off. It's well developed. I'd go so far as to say it's ready for testing." Leeman felt a sense of renewed purpose, a fighting spirit, keen to get on.

It took months of complex genetic research, while the government piled on the pressure.

"Contrary to some popular ideas, this is not an autoimmune disease, allergic response, or keratin overgrowth," Leeman eventually concluded. "It's a fungal mutation that we've never seen before. It's potentially deadly, poses a real threat to humanity, and it's resistant to all the antifungals currently available."

"I thought we'd ruled out fungi," said a colleague.

"Well you did, but you were wrong."

"Oh. How do you know this?"

"I've been able to isolate the organism and identify it. This concept isn't new. Pioneering doctors suggested years ago that this epidemic might be caused by a virulent fungal infection, but they were dismissed because they couldn't identify the organism.

This mutation has evaded detection for too long. The old boys in medicine might not like it, but sometimes, what they think they know is just plain wrong."

Chapter 23
Revelations

A briefing ensued with the full government committee and advisors present. Leeman addressed the group. "Colleagues and government officials, thank you all for coming. Now, we all know that healthy bacteria are an important part of the human immune system. But lesser-known microbes, often found competing for space in our bodies, are yeasts and fungi. Antibiotics kill bacteria indiscriminately, but they don't touch yeasts or their more harmful form, fungi. This provides an opportunity for parasitic organisms like pathogenic fungi to take over.

"Our bodies are a battleground for dominance between healthy strains of bacteria, and their opponents - pathogenic fungi and disease causing bacteria. Usually our immune system kills off these bad guys and keeps this balance in check, but my research has revealed that the epidemic of disease we're seeing is caused by a pathogenic fungal infection, which has evaded detection using traditional diagnostic methods."

"How is that so?" said a gentleman on the board. "How could we miss this for so long?"

"Progress has been held back by problems with current technologies, and by a general reluctance to acknowledge that fungal infections can cause a problem in otherwise healthy individuals. The bottom line is that researchers haven't been looking for it, or those who have, have been dismissed too quickly. So when existing technologies showed no fungal infection present, or dismissed positive results as contamination, we were all too ready to accept that. But let's not dwell on the past - at least we've identified it now."

"What makes you so sure that the new technology is giving correct results?"

"The volume of information contained in a genome sequence is vast and there can be problems with interpretation. Sometimes it's hard to see the forest for the trees, and a lot of the information is poorly understood. Significant information may be dismissed. It's complex. This new technology enables us to see what's going on more clearly, and to separate different strands of information, to get a clearer picture."

"OK. So why has this epidemic happened now?"

"I have a theory on that." He flicked through his papers and then continued. "In recent years, antibacterial drugs have become more widely available than before - in a large part, because of new medicines developed by my former team at Cother Pharmaceuticals. However, the widespread use of these drugs, combined with a cultural shift towards consuming *hot caffeine* – a fungal product – for recreation, has tipped the balance of microbes in favour of a virulent strain of fungi.

"This pathogenic strain, which I call Morbid Kaylmycotopa, is now infecting people around the world. The disease is caused by a mutation of the Kaylmycotopa fungi, commonly known as *hot caffeine.* Extracts of Kaylmycotopa are used in Smooth cream, and the oral antibiotic. We need to withdraw these products from sale and ban *hot caffeine* as a recreational drug, to get the best chance of beating this disease. I know this will be unpopular, but that's my considered opinion."

"What about the diseases that have been cured by the new antibiotic drugs? If we stop using them, people will die!" The gentleman looked gravely concerned.

"Perhaps there could be some exceptions, but the widespread use of these drugs, is contributing to the current outbreak."

"There will be an outcry from people using these you know!"

"I know, but there's no point pretending we don't know what's happening. My research shows that the epidemic is caused by these drugs, and by the recreational use of *hot caffeine*. Put simply, our lifestyles now involve many people consuming a dangerous fungus, for recreation or medicine, while simultaneously overwhelming our body's ability to fight off fungal disease."

There was a murmur and a sense of disquiet in the room, as people digested the information, and foresaw the overwhelming challenges ahead. Some disagreed with Leeman's conclusions, shaking their heads and rolling their eyes.

Responding to their scepticism, Leeman continued, "Bacteria have been seen as the greater threat for many decades, but today, the tables have turned. It is now fungal infections that present the greatest threat to humanity. It's been a long-standing error within the medical profession that fungal infections are not taken seriously unless you're already extremely ill. But my research shows that this disease, which causes a crippling skin condition, dizziness, and exhaustion, is caused by a fungal mutation.

"These infections may begin as mild and superficial, but the fungi can mutate and spread. They ferment sugars, just like yeast ferments beer, leading to some people feeling drunk when they've not had a drink, and they can cause a whole host of digestive problems. They cause skin discolouration, soreness and lesions. Some people get raised plaques where the body responds by trying to replace diseased skin with new growth."

Sceptics in the audience seemed less than convinced, but Leeman continued, "Fungi are incredibly adaptable - they quickly mutate and become resistant to treatments. This means it can be very difficult to eradicate them. With this fungi's remarkable resistance and adaptability, there isn't going to be a quick fix. It's showing signs of spreading more quickly, and becoming more deadly."

"So what do you suggest? Where do we go from here?"

"Well, it's resistant to all existing medication, but a lot of recent research has been looking at enhancing the immune system so that the body is able to fight infection naturally. So perhaps a two-pronged approach could be developed – new antifungals, combined with immune-boosting meds. It's just going to take some time, which is obviously in short supply at the moment, but with the backing of the government committee, we can work fast!"

"Aren't some researchers working on this already?"

"Yes, but very few resources have been allocated to researching pathogenic fungal infections as a possible cause. Those scientists who've been looking at it have been up against ridicule and lack of funding. So we're not where we should be on the antifungal research, and it's hard to do immunological research when you don't know what you're dealing with."

The committee members took the reports away to digest the evidence, but initial reactions were that there was no way the government would want to ban the country's most successful drugs, which had bought so much investment into the country, and put the country on the world stage. What about all the good they'd done? All the diseases they'd cured? There would also be huge public resistance to a ban on processed *hot caffeine* and it would be impossible to enforce a ban on raw unprocessed Kayl. The challenges ahead felt insurmountable.

Chapter 24
Resistance

Leeman's theories were leaked to the press and ended up on the evening news, with medical experts quick to dismiss his ideas and say he was considered 'eccentric' and should not be taken seriously. But some of the people suffering from the disease were keen to know more.

"Could Morbid Kaylmycotopa have anything to do with Jessica's bipolar?" asked Eve when she next had an appointment with Leeman.

"Yes, it certainly could," he said. "The fungal toxins will be circulating in her blood stream, making her feel bad, tired... perhaps depressed, and of course, it's natural to feel blue when you're unwell."

"That's really enlightening."

"The low periods could be punctuated with periods of mania if the fungi are messing with her brain chemicals. I have seen people with bipolar respond very positively to antifungal treatment in the past, but that was with different strains and existing treatments. There is nothing on the market that would eradicate this particular infection right now, so I can only recommend a low-carbohydrate diet which may reduce the severity of her symptoms, and she should avoid *hot caffeine* or Kayl."

Eve nodded. "OK. Well that gives us something to try. Thank you. Do keep us updated on progress won't you?"

"Don't worry. I'll keep in touch, and if you're willing, you can be involved in any new drug trials for promising antifungal medications."

"Oh yes please. We'd like to hear about anything new."

*   *   *

While Eve, Jessica, and other sufferers were desperate to see progress, they thought any news was good news. But government officials weren't at all convinced by David Leeman's research or his conclusions. Meanwhile, the medical profession were up in arms. A huge lobby of vested interests quickly arose to invalidate his research and discredit him as an expert. The opponents were many; the ridicule, relentless.

"This is unknown and untested technology," said one government official to Leeman, after speaking to his medical colleagues. "You've used unproven methods to draw fanciful conclusions that fly in the face of medical knowledge. Your technology is flawed. My esteemed medical colleagues are certain that this is not a fungus. Your study design is flawed! And to top it all, you've spoken to the patients about it!"

Leeman protested, "It was leaked to the evening news! Not by me, I hasten to add. The patients knew about the development before I'd seen them. Besides, these were the patients I'd used in the study, so keeping them in the dark would have been morally wrong. They came to us for help, and I told them what I'd discovered… I'd still like to run the tests on a larger sample group to confirm my theory."

"I'm afraid that won't be possible Dr Leeman. The other researchers want you removed from the team. They say your methods are unorthodox and your conclusions, fanciful. They insist that you cannot get a chronic fungal infection unless you have immune suppression – which these patients did not have. Routine tests show each patient to be free from fungal disease. Your colleagues have even suggested that some of these patients are imagining some symptoms and you're fuelling their paranoia with silly ideas."

"The creamy yellowing patches on these people's skin are not in their mind," Leeman said plainly. "I'm disappointed by all this negativity and contempt. I've only been back a few months and you're already dismissing everything I have to say."

"It's not me sir. It's the educated opinion of the esteemed experts on the research team."

"They're just too narrow minded to see what's right in front of their eyes. I completely believe in the results of my work, and the fact that no one else has been able to draw any conclusions just shows that my 'unorthodox' approaches are well overdue."

"I'm afraid your colleagues do not agree Dr Leeman. There is a perception that your mind is so traumatised by the unfortunate events in your life, that this is clouding your judgement. Perhaps you've been brought back to work prematurely. The team want to look at ways of curbing abnormal growths, perhaps with surgery, and treating keratin overgrowth. They do not want to put resources into antifungal medications, or immune-boosters. We have excellent immunotherapy techniques already, and they've proven to be completely ineffective. The team cannot see any validity in your judgements or your arguments... And I'm afraid I agree. We'd like you to go on indefinite gardening leave. We'll take over the research and deal with the patients from here on."

Leeman was furious, "You're all wrong you know! You're facing the biggest health crisis in living history and you're dismissing the only person who's worked out what's going on! You're crazy! This is serious. You can't be messing about in denial at a time like this! Face it - this fungus is challenging your beliefs and you need to open your eyes and see what is staring you in the face."

"I don't wish to discuss this any further. Good day Dr Leeman," the official got up and left.

Fuming, Leeman went home, slept badly, and continued to brood.

*   *   *

Terry's appointment at the hospital dermatology department arrived and she was keen to hear what the specialist had to say. A pretty woman in her 40s with short brown hair, came out of the consulting room and called her in. They shook hands.

"I'm Dr Long, your dematologist," she said.

"Hi," said Terry.

"Now let's take a look," said the Doctor. "Do you want to tell me all about it?"

Terry rolled up her sleeves and explained the problem - how it seemed to be exacerbated by Smooth and how it had worsened in recent weeks.

"And it's all over your body?"

"It's patchy, but yes. Afraid so. It's very unpleasant, as you can imagine."

The dermatologist looked at the lesions and sores and nodded knowingly. "Hmmm," she said, and scribbled lots of notes. Then she sat up and confirmed that Terry had the same mystery illness as so many others. "I'm afraid there's no known cure," she said.

"But it's not all doom and gloom. There are drugs, lotions, and deep moisturisers, which can help you to manage the symptoms. Let's try them, and meet again in a month to review the situation," she suggested. Terry agreed, feeling quite positive. She returned home with a bag full of goodies, which she hoped would relieve her symptoms. And to be fair, they did help quite a lot, making her appearance much better so she could go back to work after a short break.

Chapter 25
A *Hot Caffeine* Ban

Despite overwhelming opposition to Leeman's calls to ban *hot caffeine*, evidence was emerging that the drug had mind-altering effects, which were not just temporary. Permanent damage to the brain could be caused by prolonged use. As evidence of its damaging effects mounted, it became clear that *hot caffeine* could cause lower IQ, poor concentration, loss of self-control, and a greater propensity to addiction. The British government ran a campaign to discourage its use.

Terry turned on BBC News. "The Department for Health is warning that unless there's a voluntary reduction in consumption of *hot caffeine* there's a risk of people across the country experiencing a decline in cognitive ability and lower intelligence," said the reporter. "Evidence is emerging that consuming *hot caffeine* regularly might be worse than smoking, in terms of its negative impact on health."

Not good, she thought. *A lot of people are mildly addicted!*

The government campaign had little effect - people carried on as before. So eventually, the sale of the processed *hot caffeine* and its by-products in supermarkets, grocery stores, and bars, was made illegal in Britain, and consumption of the raw fungus was banned. It seemed like the responsible thing to do in Parliament, but the decision didn't go down well on the streets and many people ignored it.

Angry protests formed outside Parliament, but the anger died down when people realised there was no enforcement of the law, and a thriving black market had sprung up to meet their needs.

"It's annoying that I can't pick it up in my weekly shop," a customer complained to Terry in the shop.

"Well they say it's no good for you. Makes you stupid." Terry grinned.

"Neither is alcohol, but that's never stopped us from enjoying it," said the customer. She wasn't seeing the funny side.

"That's true."

Many people did respect the ban - not wishing to do themselves or their family harm. But others were learning to prepare their own, or were eating Kayl raw from the garden. The authorities were fighting a losing battle. It was virtually impossible to police and the processed commercial products were still available in Continental Europe, so many people just ordered it online.

Jessica was told to avoid *hot caffeine*, but she was craving it badly. She had grown to hate the side effects of her bipolar medication – a dull sense of nothingness. So eventually she stopped taking it and started to consume raw Kayl straight from the garden, ignoring doctors and government advice to avoid it.

Without her medicinal drugs, she started acting weird again, suffering from delusions and having panic attacks - but at least she felt alive. As much as Eve hated it, she felt that Jessica needed more specialist help with her bipolar and would be better served by an inpatient clinic.

"Mum, I'm so frightened," Jessica wailed, "What's happening to me?" Eve pulled her close and embraced her tightly. "I love you Jess. We'll get through this."

"I just want to die," Jess confessed.

Eve understood. Poor Jessica's appearance had suffered dreadfully with the discolouration, creamy patches, and sores. It was a miserable existence and little wonder she was depressed. She was riddled with self-doubt, had chronic fatigue, a bloated tummy, and dizziness as if she were drunk. She hated the drugs that had such unpleasant side-effects. It was easy to understand why she was abandoning them and finding solace in her old favourite, Kayl from the garden.

"Jess, I don't think you understand. David Leeman says your consumption of *hot caffeine* may have been partially responsible for the disease."

"I do understand - and everyone else thinks he's wrong. I need it mum. To calm me."

"That sounds like an addiction, sweetheart."

"Perhaps it is, perhaps it isn't - as long as I feel better, I don't really care."

In recent weeks, however, her coordination seemed to have been affected – whether it was due to the illness, the drugs, or Kayl, it was hard to tell.

Jessica's emotions were overwhelming her. "Remember me as I was before mum," she cried. "When I die, I don't want to be remembered like this."

"You're not going to die – you're going to get better," Eve insisted, tears in her eyes.

Jess agreed to try a clinic. "I can visit you every day," said Eve, "But these specialists will be able to help you manage your health issues better than I ever could, and once they've got you feeling better, you can come home. We can continue the health regime here. Think positive. This is a good opportunity!" Jess looked frightened and confused, but reluctantly agreed. Things couldn't go on the way they were.

On the first day at the clinic, Eve was willing to stay all day to help her settle in, but there were a bunch of other new people and she felt it would be better for Jessica, not to have her mother hanging around. They said tearful goodbyes, and Eve left Jessica in the expert hands of the clinicians.

Days turned to weeks and Jessica received regular therapy, nutritional supplements, an optimal diet, relaxation techniques and group talk sessions. Her erratic behaviour continued, but she went through periods of remission – sometimes she seemed to be getting better. Other times, she seemed to get worse, screaming, cutting herself, and talking of suicide. There was a lot of work to do.

Chapter 26
In Search of Healing

Like Jessica, Terry was struggling with health problems. She'd got a collection of creams and potions, some of which relieved her symptoms. However, the drugs only went so far. They were better than nothing, but she really wanted a cure.

Looking for a chance of deeper healing, Terry saw an advert for a Christian faith healing convention in London. It was free to attend, and everyone was invited to go along for a blessing, to experience spiritual awakening, and to know the healing power of God for themselves. Well it couldn't do any harm, she thought, and diarised the date.

The healing convention was held on a massive stage in the open air, in Hyde Park. There were large screens on either side of the stage, a full PA system, huge crowds, and a vibrant atmosphere, full of hope.

A preacher stepped onto the stage, "Meet your host, Jack Hawk!" He waved. "Hello all! We're here to immerse you in the power of the Holy Spirit, and make you well! Let's get going!" Very quickly, haunting music filled the air, creating a surreal environment. "Shut your eyes and let the spirit of the Lord wash over you. Immerse yourself in His presence and feel His love come upon you. Ask for healing and focus your mind entirely on Him. Let nothing else interrupt your thoughts."

Easy for you to say, Terry thought, as her mind wandered all over the place. The crowd was fascinating, with some people clearly suffering from the early stages of the disease, and others disabled, or seeking healing from other afflictions. A group of people in eccentric dress caught her eye. They had multi-coloured hair and rock punk-style outfits. There were also businessmen and women, tramps - literally people from all walks of life.

She stood there trying to focus on God, but uninvited thoughts and doubts kept entering her head. She felt a bit stupid as she hadn't had an active Christian faith for a long time, and it would be embarrassing if her friends spotted her. But it was unlikely that any of them would come, unless they too, were seeking healing, of course. The disease was getting to everyone these days. No one was safe.

"Submit your whole being to the creator," the preacher continued, "Let him shower you with blessings." He reached up towards the heavens, arms raised as if to embrace an invisible force. Happiness and faith radiated from his face.

His monotonous voice continued like a guided meditation, echoing around the park, enchanting the audience. His words were soothing and reassuring. *This is so relaxing*, thought Terry, as she chilled, open to the power of suggestion. Entranced by his powerful words, people were carried along in a wave of emotion.

"Sob, sob," came a sound nearby.

"Thank you God!" rang voices, as people embraced the experience.

The preacher's voice hit a crescendo. "Someone's been healed - right here, right now. I can sense it. Praise the Lord!"

"Praise the Lord!" came replies from the crowd. People fainted - apparently filled by the Holy Spirit. Others cried tears of joy.

The preacher continued, "Those people who want to receive the gift of healing, come to the front to receive prayers. We'll light candles to the glory of God. Ask for healing and forgiveness." Terry was shaking. *Should I go up? Can I be healed?* Almost involuntarily, her legs started towards the front, where people were waiting to pray with the afflicted. She felt nervous, but was compelled to step forward to receive healing.

"Continue to focus your mind on Him alone. He wants to cleanse you of all evil. Surrender your body to him and allow him to purify you completely. Place all your trust in Him," said the preacher.

Terry stepped up and a woman led her to a pit beside the stage and asked, "What's your name love?"

"Terry."

"Are you suffering from the disease?" Terry nodded. No further explanation was needed.

The woman laid her hands on Terry's head and started to pray, "Lord, banish the demon from inside Terry. Make her immune system strong, and her body powerful. Give her the strength and

104

reassurance in your love and compassion, to know that you can, and will, heal her." The woman started to speak strangely in a language that Terry had never heard before. It continued for ages, while the preacher on the stage continued to talk of God's healing and compassion.

When the event finished Terry said her goodbyes to the woman who had prayed for her, "Keep your faith - healing will come," the woman promised. But as the weeks and months passed, healing didn't come. *Maybe my faith isn't strong enough*, she pondered.

Terry stayed in touch with Sheila, recounting the ups and downs of her healing journey.

"What do you propose to do now?" Sheila asked.

"I don't know," she said. "I'm experimenting with different drugs, but there doesn't seem to be a lot that the dermatologist can offer me. Perhaps I'll try a local spiritualist church where the emphasis is less on my personal faith, and more on their own capacity for healing. I'm not going to let this disease get the better of me."

Sheila looked concerned. "Be careful dabbling with the occult - there are things we don't understand." But Terry was keen to dabble in anything that might help!

At the local spiritualist church, the atmosphere was informal and the people she met were warm and chatty. Terry got a cup of tea and sat down. There were no obvious signs of people afflicted by the disease. Feeling curious, she asked a gentleman sitting next to her, "Doesn't anyone else here have the skin problems that are going around?"

"Oh yes!'" he laughed, "Most of us are afflicted to a greater or lesser degree, but we've all come to terms with it, without healing, and none are so advanced that the disease is immediately obvious to others. Our acceptance of the situation seems to keep our stress levels down, which slows the progression of the disease."

"I don't understand. Do you mean you can't heal it, or you don't want to?"

"I suppose it must be difficult for you to understand, but I'll try to explain. Since our time with this fellowship, we have all seen the spirits during séances. The afterlife is wonderful. One acquires a heavenly existence that brings eternal happiness. The full glory of the afterlife is beyond our comprehension but we understand enough to realise that death is not something to be feared. Death is in fact, a new beginning with Christ and something that we all look forward to. So the disease you see, is just a stepping stone to our final destiny – paradise with our Saviour. If God has chosen to take us, then we are ready, and we don't want to fight it, but that doesn't mean we can't help you, if you don't feel that your time has come yet. Perhaps you do need more time on this earth, to work out your own faith."

Terry wasn't sure what to think and wondered if they were all as nutty as a fruitcake, but slowing the progression of the disease was an amazing achievement. The man stood up and offered her his hand. "Come and join our séance," he said. "It's about to begin." With nothing to lose, she decided to take part.

They sat in a solemn circle and a male medium called upon the spirits. "Is anybody there? Make yourself known." He sat quietly for a moment, then suddenly jerked rigidly and started murmuring strange sounds. The fellowship looked entranced. A distant voice fell from his mouth – it was a soft female voice and one gentleman recognised it.

"Margaret!" the old man cried.

"Hello Norman," the woman's voice was soft and gentle, not at all like the medium himself, "How are you my love?"

"I'm all right my darling. I've got a disease so I'll be joining you soon," he looked happy and peaceful.

"You'll love it here," the velvety voice seemed full of happiness, free from anxiety. "The afterlife is pure paradise."

"Oh Margaret, it's wonderful to hear your voice."

As they talked, Terry looked around the room, curious, sceptical, and looking for logical explanations as to how this was happening. Perhaps the medium was just a good actor. That voice was amazing!

"I have to leave you now Norman..."

"Not already!" the old man suddenly became distressed, "Margaret? Margaret?" But she was gone.

The medium's own voice returned, "Someone's disbelief has severed my connection to the spirit world. Please doubters - do not spoil this for others. Put aside your doubt and believe what you see and hear. Your senses are not deceiving you. There is nothing underhand going on here. If you cannot put your disbelief

106

aside, then please leave the group and allow us to continue without hindrance."

Terry blushed. No one left. The medium continued.

He entered another trance and started to sway. Then a little girl's voice came out of nowhere.

"Hello mummy!" It was the voice of a child.

"Hello Tammy." The child's mother.

"Don't be sad mummy. There are lots of toys here and I have many friends."

"That's great darling," mum remarked tearfully, yet smiling. "I miss you so much."

"When you die you can come here too and we'll never be parted."

"Are you well cared for Tammy?"

"Yes mummy. Everything is beautiful here. You mustn't worry about me."

Mother and daughter talked for a few minutes, but the medium became tired and the communication became more distant before ceasing altogether.

"I'll need ten minutes of rest, and then we can call on the spirits for healing," he said. The group dispersed, getting drinks and using the toilet, then they reconvened for a healing séance.

The regular participants joined hands and started to chant. "Come to us, spirits of healing. Heal our bodies, heal our souls." Terry sat between them quietly. Holding hands but not chanting. A forceful wind blew outwards from the centre of the circle, almost sending one member toppling off her chair. "Huh!" Terry gasped. The invisible power present in the room sent shivers down her spine.

"Move into the centre of the circle Terry," the medium instructed. "The spirits of healing are here to help you." A light wind continued to rush inside the circle and certainly there was something odd there. Terry was nervous and paused.

"The spirits can only heal you if you're willing to step up and join them," pressed the medium.

What on earth is going on! she thought, as she reluctantly stepped into the centre of the windy circle. *What am I doing?! Is it safe? Where is this wind coming from?* The circle closed around her.

"Now let healing begin!" the medium bellowed. He stood up, holding his arms in the air majestically.

The wind rushed through Terry's hair and she felt strange sensations as unseen things brushed past. She turned her head, eyes opened wide, but could only see flickers of light in the wind, her own hair blowing about in her face. She felt a tingling sensation on her back but could see nothing to cause it. She squinted as a gust of wind blew into her face. Then the medium started moaning – a strange sound, a varying pitch. The tingling sensation moved deeper into Terry's back, and then started to prick – a quite unpleasant experience. *Is this the healing process? I hope it's over soon!* she thought.

The sensations stopped suddenly. The wind stopped, and the medium laughed. Through his mouth, flowed other voices speaking strange tongues. *This is so weird, horrible,* she thought. Her mind raced, afraid. *I feel stupid and scared, and I need to get out of here!* She pushed through the circle, ran towards the exit, and didn't stop running until she got home.

Terry wept bitterly on her bed. If only she'd listened to Sheila. She just hadn't thought it through. Her back ached, so she retired for a long hot bath. As she pulled off her T shirt, she could see that nothing had changed – the creamy growth was as bad as ever, and as she prodded her skin, it was painful too.

*   *   *

Stephen's condition had deteriorated. The area around his eyes were big creamy blotches now and his mates called him 'panda'. It wasn't funny. He was depressed. No one fancied him any more. He looked in the mirror. *I hate this.* His dark brown eyes looked beady beneath the puffy skin. He'd even been turned down by a prostitute. *Boy, I am so depressed!*

Chapter 27
Emptiness

Leeman's life without Jenny or meaningful work felt depressingly empty. Everything seemed pointless. Years had passed since the murder, but his bitter hatred towards Alex Turnbull hadn't faded. *It's about time they brought back the death sentence and made the punishment fit the crime.*

He pondered his purpose in life and felt terrible. *Things are going from bad to worse. I've been dismissed from the research project. Got no respect. My therapist says focus on the present, be positive, but how am I supposed to do that? I need work! The worst thing is, they're still running around like headless chickens, denying the cause of the disease. Idiots.*

He found solace in a support group for the bereaved, and a group of activists who believed in the fungi theory to explain the recent epidemic of disease. They believed that the creamy patches and yellowy growths on the skin were caused by a fungus. The dizziness, drunk feeling, and chronic tiredness were all recognised symptoms of such an infection. The cure would usually be strict dietary guidelines and an antifungal or two, but that's where the theory fell apart, because the disease was totally resistant to antifungal drugs, and dietary interventions were unreliable and didn't always work.

It all made complete sense to Leeman though. He decided to meet with members of the group and became involved in their work, channelling his passion into helping them spread the message, lobbying the government, and trying to get influential people on board. It helped. It gave him a sense of purpose and stopped him from feeling so blue.

Chapter 28
Newfield

Jessica's time at Newfield Psychiatric Clinic was warm and comfortable - they had strict regimes but a caring atmosphere. The clinic stood next door to Newfield Psychiatric Hospital, a secure facility designed for the treatment of offenders. It was home to Alex Turnbull, who had been incarcerated there for a couple of years, after murdering Jenny Leeman. Alex was receiving ongoing psychiatric treatment for his violent outbursts, but the treatments were having little effect and he was still considered to be dangerous. Other patients had similar temperaments, backgrounds and problems. Some doctors and psychiatrists worked at both institutions, but the clients of the two establishments never met.

Patients like Jessica at the clinic were suffering from a variety of conditions - bipolar, depression, eating disorders and self harm. Jessica found the environment strange but supportive. It was going to take some getting used to.

In the secure hospital next door, inmates were locked up for parts of the day and let out into supervised communal areas at other times. Strict regimes were followed, but today, trouble was afoot. "Hey, warden!" called inmate Dodge from his cell. "I've heard that this irritating itch could be life-threatening. Is that true?"

"It's true! I've seen the newspaper reports!" shouted another patient down the corridor. "Total bloody disgrace. It's been allowed to spread around here, and we're all kept in the dark!"

"Listen up," shouted Warden Bob. "No one here has more than a superficial infection. That's not something you need to worry about. If anyone had a bad infection, they'd be moved to new quarters for treatment. This little itch - it might just go away on its own. It's nothing to worry about."

"Bullshit! I've had it for months!" said Dodge. "Jezza's had his for years! His skin's discoloured."

"Yeah!" said Jezza.

"Yeah!" a rousing chorus from other cells.

"We're monitoring it," said the warden. "Jezza's not considered high risk or contagious."

"What a load of tripe. You don't care about us!" shouted Dodge.

"You can raise it with your doctors if you're worried."

"And I will!"

They rattled their bars, shouted and jeered. The warden walked away.

Staff had taken a few precautions to protect themselves when dealing with patients, but they weren't seriously concerned about contagion on the wing.

However, when the inmates were let out of their cells for lunch, they went on a protest, fuelled by rage and fear.

"Tear the place apart!" shouted Dodge. "We'll show them!" Wardens restrained him, but other patients were on the rampage and soon the guards had lost control.

Matron was more respected than most, but even she was struggling to make herself heard. "Listen to me! It's not that bad!" Alex and Jezza stopped vandalising the furniture and turned to look at her. "No one in here has anything more than a superficial infection," she continued. "*That* is *not* life-threatening! It's not even thought to be contagious. It's NOTHING to worry about. Scientists are working around the clock to find a cure, and when they do, there'll be treatments available. Not one of you is going to die. You just have to be patient!"

They turned away. They didn't care. Half these people were crazy and the other half didn't give a toss! They trashed the place, beating up anyone who got in their way.

Initially, only two patients inside Newfield Psychiatric Hospital had been infected, but now many were showing signs of disease - pale spots, some itching, complaining about discomfort.

"Why were we locked up with infected people!" shouted Dodge, still battling with his captors. "We're all going to bloody die now!"

"You're not going to die," repeated Matron.

"You treat us like shit!" said Jezza as he ran off to create more anarchy. Patients charged around the communal areas, smashing

111

things, throwing anything that wasn't nailed down, and creating an uproar.

Lights were smashed, chairs destroyed, tables upturned, curtains torn down. Plants toppled, compost across the floor. Some staff tried to stop the rioting, putting patients back in their cells. The situation was contained but not controlled.

Suddenly there was an enormous crash and smoke billowed into the lobby. A fire had broken out. Patients watched in horror and delight, as flames crept up the curtains.

"Call the fire brigade and get to the assembly points!" screamed a young nurse. She pressed a button unlocking the internal doors so that staff and patients could move away from the fire to other parts of the hospital.

But as the fire took hold, the smoke was getting everywhere, seeping through closed doors, creating a real risk for those trapped inside the building.

"We need to get out!" said the nurse. "This place is filling with smoke. Where's Mrs Halton? She has the only set of keys to the external doors!"

No one answered. A pause. "Is she upstairs?" someone suggested.

"I'll go and take a look," Warden Bob headed up the stairs to find her.

"I've called the fire brigade," shouted Warden Mike. "They won't be long." He coughed on the insidious smoke.

"Mrs Halton's a total control freak," said the nurse. "It's all very well liking to keep the keys secure, but this obsessive carry-on doesn't work in an emergency! It must be a breach of health and safety rules!"

"Can we leave by the staff entrance?" suggested Mike.

"It's not secure. Against protocol..."

"I can live with breaking protocol in an emergency," said Mike.

"Hang on," She went to check the route and returned quickly. "It's also blocked by flames!"

"Shit!" Jezza piped up. "You stupid people. I can't believe you've got no protocol for emergency access to the outside. This is bloody ridiculous!"

"Well if you didn't riot and start fires, we wouldn't need protocol!" the nurse was tearful.

"OK. Calm down," said Mike. "We need to work together. The windows are barred. What about fire escapes?"

"They were bolted because patients were trying to escape into the therapy garden without supervision."

"Yes, but we should have keys."

"Erm, I think they're with Mrs Halton too?"

"OK. Health and safety would have a field day here! We need to find Mrs Halton!"

"Bob's on the case."

Mike and Jezza tried to tackle the flames with extinguishers, but it was hopeless. The heat was too much. Black smoke billowed through the halls. People coughed and spluttered, choking.

"The devil is calling!" screamed a schizophrenic patient. "He's come for me!" He jumped up, and danced from foot to foot towards the flames, then ran straight into the fire wailing and screaming as the flames licked his clothes and engulfed his body. There was silence again as the smell of burning flesh filled the air.

Anarchy forgotten, patients and staff stuck together, heading to the other end of the cell block, staying low, where the smoke was thinner.

"Mrs Halton!" Warden Bob was calling, coughing, as he charged through smoke filled corridors. He darted into thick black clouds and eventually turned up at the top of the stairs, choking and barely visible through the smoke, with a body heaped over his shoulder. Mrs Halton's key chain clinked in his hand. He ran downstairs quickly, called through to those who'd moved away from the fire, and opened the doors to the outdoors. Black smoke rushed outside, swiftly followed by everyone from the hospital. They stood together in the therapy garden and coughed to clear their lungs. Alex collapsed on the ground, exhausted.

* * *

In the clinic next door, evacuation procedures had also begun, in case the fire were to spread to the next building. The two buildings were separated by a tall fence, topped with barbed-wire but they stood very close to one another. The billowing smoke from the hospital created a smog in the grounds of the clinic next door. Jessica ran down the stairs, heading straight for the nearest exit. Staff and other patients all made haste for the safety of the outdoors.

"Stand well back from the smoke!" said clinic staff as they rounded everyone up. They checked everyone off a list. "Now wait in the garden, well back from the smoke."

A siren sounded, 'nee-naa, nee-naa!' The fire brigade pulled up outside the hospital, unravelled their hoses, and started to tackle the flames. As black smoke poured into the sky, staff and patients with blackened faces and clothes were checked for smoke inhalation and burns. Mrs Halton, who'd blacked out, was given oxygen. Some of the inmates wanted to make a bid for freedom, but solid fencing, heavy gates and a large police presence thwarted any ideas they might have had for a quick getaway.

* * *

Eventually the fire was brought under control, but as the flames were slowly extinguished, it became clear that the hospital building was uninhabitable. Alternative accommodation had to be found. High-risk patients were moved to other secure hospitals, while low-risk patients were sent to police cells for a short stay. Tall fencing was erected around Newfield Psychiatric Clinic, and Jessica looked out, wondering what was going on. "Why is fencing going up?" she asked a member of staff.

"They're putting some of the inmates from next door into accommodation on this site," she explained. "You don't need to worry. They're low risk offenders and you'll probably never meet them. The fences are for them, not you. You can come and go as you please."

"Can mum still visit?"

"Yes, of course."

That was reassuring.

Some inmates were eventually moved from police cells into a dilapidated wing of Newfield Psychiatric Clinic, which had been out of use for years but would provide secure temporary accommodation and give the authorities some time to work out a more permanent solution. Meanwhile, incarcerated patients would have access to the psychiatric services they needed. Tightened security was put in place. Bars on the windows kept the inmates inside.

Prisoners were mostly kept separate from voluntary patients at the clinic, but there were occasions when they met, using shared services and facilities. Alex and Jessica met while waiting to see their respective therapists.

She sat down in the waiting room, saw him looking at her, and smiled. He looked nice - rugged and handsome, but quite a lot older than her.

"Hi," he said. "You got an appointment today?"

"Yes, just my regular therapist."

"Are they good here?"

"I find mine helpful," she said.

"I'm new, so it's my first time."

"Oh. Are you from next door?"

"Yes. Awful thing that fire. Don't know how it started."

"So much smoke!"

"Horrible."

They met at therapy regularly and became friends. She liked his sense of humour and his passion for good causes. He seemed a good kind. Despite the generational differences, it didn't seem to be a barrier to their friendship.

Chapter 29
Mockery and Dismissal

It was time for the government-appointed committee of scientists to report their findings. Jack Payne was a lead researcher on the team. He went to meet the health minister, shook hands and took a seat.

"So where have we got to?" asked the MP.

Payne looked saddened, "The disease is showing no signs of remission, as you know."

The MP nodded gravely.

"Many medics have put their patients on the new generation antibiotics, to see if an undetected bacterial infection is the cause, but in most cases these medicines haven't helped. If anything, they've made it worse."

"OK. Well, what leads have we got?"

"We're inclined to think it's an immune response to something in the environment. That's entirely theoretical, but we've found no evidence of infection."

"So how come it's spreading?"

"We're not sure. It might be that whatever is triggering the response is more widespread in the environment than it was before. Alternatively, it might be caused by a parasite... or perhaps there's some infectious microbe. We've run a lot of tests and not found anything, but it's not impossible."

"You've not found evidence of parasites or nasty microbes?"

"No."

"Is there anything firm that you can tell me?"

"It's been a mixed bag, sir. We've had people complaining of minor irritations, but been unable to find anything wrong with them. Some cases might be age-related. We also suspect some people have hidden allergies that are causing their skin problems."

"What do you think people might be allergic to?" said the MP.

"Well, that's the challenge. We don't know! All we can do is ask them to keep diaries and monitor their conditions. Administering antihistamines helps in some cases. In some instances, the body seems to be attacking itself, creating plaques and sores on the skin. This points to an autoimmune disease, but the only treatments for this are immunosuppressive drugs, which in trials have made the symptoms worse. So at the moment, we're not recommending that as a course of treatment."

"Hmmm. I don't want to create further panic, so I'd suggest you keep that theory to yourselves."

Payne nodded. "We are finding treatments that numb pain and soothe discomfort are helpful in managing the disease, so there's some progress in treating it."

"OK. Well keep up the good work," said the MP. "Thank you for the update."

*   *   *

Back in the NHS, hospitals were seeing an increase in serious cases of disease, some exacerbated by underlying conditions. The worst patients were transported to specialist treatment centres, relieving pressure on hospitals and containing the spread.

Meanwhile, medics were tired of people turning up at surgeries and A&E Departments complaining about mild symptoms, like itchy blotchy skin, which they felt could be treated at home, with over-the-counter medicines.

"People with severe disease are being treated in specialist facilities, where the situation is contained and under control," said one General Practitioner on Morning TV. "There is no need for anyone to panic. Those in hospitals and in treatment centres are doing well receiving specialist care."

"Some are dying," said the presenter.

"Yes, it's true that some people with underlying conditions have passed away, but those with the greatest need are receiving the best possible help. We are doing everything we can for them."

"What about those still coming forward with symptoms?"

"We'd like people with mild symptoms to treat themselves. We are stretched to the limit and many of the patients coming to the surgery now, have nothing clinically wrong with them. Some have a little keratin overgrowth, a sign of skin irritation, damage or stress. It's quite normal and will probably go away on its own if they stop worrying about it!

"Others have some skin discolouring, which isn't going to kill them. Lots of people are complaining of chronic fatigue and digestive disturbances. But who doesn't get tired sometimes, especially when they're lying awake, worrying about an epidemic? And if they stopped eating junk food, they'd probably find their digestive problems miraculously disappeared! We've become a nation of hypochondriacs!"

"Mild cases can become severe if left untreated though," said the presenter.

"Yes, of course, and the people in clinics and hospitals are receiving excellent treatment for the advanced stages of disease, but they still represent a minority. A lot of younger people seem better able to control their symptoms with over-the-counter medication. We're working hard with those patients who have serious problems, researching treatments and doing our very best, but it's all under control. There is no need for alarm."

He spoke for many in the medical profession, who were frustrated by the numbers of people with mild cases putting pressure on NHS services.

"What are you doing to help the worried well?" asked the presenter.

"We're putting patients on antidepressants to brighten their mood," he said disdainfully. "We can also recommend creams, which are now available without a prescription to people experiencing symptoms. If symptoms worsen we'll send patients to a dermatologist who might recommend other treatments to help them manage their discomfort. Others are referred to an allergy clinic, if we think there might be an underlying allergy. Waiting lists are long though, so we prefer to try over-the-counter remedies and antihistamines where possible."

* * *

"I still think they've got it wrong," said David Leeman to a friend and activist, Rob, who believed in his fungi theory.

"Too right they have! The evidence is clear. This is caused by a fungal organism! No doubt about it."

"I feel awful though - I think I'm partly responsible for the outbreak. By developing that powerful new antibiotic, I've taken the war between healthy bacteria and pathogenic fungi to a whole new level. Not in a good way."

"It's not your fault," said Rob. "Loads of pharmaceutical companies were working on new antibiotics for years before your success, and don't forget about the impact of Kayl - or *hot caffeine* as it's popularly known. That's spread the disease faster than anything you've done, because people won't leave it alone."

"True. But my drugs wiped out armies of healthy bacteria that might have protected people from the disease. They were central to people's immune systems, and they've been decimated."

"Well the medics seem to think the microbiome recovers and are still arguing that point, so don't beat yourself up mate. It was going to happen one day. Now, we just need to get the message out there - try to convince people to treat it like a fungal infection. It's the only way they'll ever get rid of it."

"I don't know..." he sighed, feeling tired and a bit overwhelmed by the situation. "Antifungals don't work. There's not really a good treatment."

"No. But we both know there are loads of other approaches to harnessing the power of your immune system, that might get rid of this wretched disease."

"Possibly. I wish they hadn't taken me off the research team."

"Total bloody idiots mate. Don't take it personally."

The antibiotics had left people open to infection. This wasn't radical - the old antibiotics had caused fungal infections too, but the easy availability of these new drugs had increased people's exposure with devastating results.

People's use of antibiotics was higher than at any previous time in human history. They were available in pills and potions, in far greater concentrations than in the past. Doctors saw them as a first line of defence, so were quick to prescribe them for numerous ailments. The new antibiotics were even starting to make their way into animal feed, to the alarm of animal rights groups who'd been protesting against routine use of traditional antibiotics in intensive farming for years. The recreational use of *hot caffeine*, a pathogenic fungus, was just the nail in the coffin. It helped the fungal pathogens to take hold and the disease to spread.

As Leeman despaired, governments, pharmaceutical companies, medics and the public, were still in denial. Research programmes looked at using immunosuppressant drugs for sores or salicylic acid creams for keratin overgrowth. But they weren't getting to the core of the problem, and sometimes they were making things worse.

* * *

Meanwhile the disease was slowly and silently spreading around the world. The pace of infection seemed to be accelerating, as people succumbed to skin problems, soreness, digestive problems, clouded thinking, depression, and terrible chronic fatigue. Vulnerable people were dying, often from secondary complications, but still there was little understanding of the true nature of the disease.

As the situation worsened, seriously ill people needed to take extended periods off work. Those that didn't get better were laid off and forced onto welfare. Mass sickness slowly became more common than good health, and employers were struggling to find staff to keep their businesses ticking over.

* * *

Leeman took his research to government officials and consulted other medics, trying to get his theories heard. But they all ignored him. His former employers, and some government figures with vested interests, were keen to shut him up. The pharmaceutical profession was doing well out of this crisis. People would try everything and anything when they got desperate. It was very profitable.

Drug companies were doing a roaring trade in drugs that reduced pain and relieved symptoms. If the suggestion got out that the wonder drugs - still selling in their billions across the globe - were perhaps in part responsible for the epidemic, the company and its associates wouldn't survive the legal battles that would surely ensue.

"Keep your mouth shut and stop pedalling myths, or you'll never work again," he was warned. But the natural health community and some who'd come round to Leeman's ideas started challenging the ethics of the government, medics and the pharmaceutical industry.

Thousands of protestors paraded through the streets of London demanding greater transparency and honesty about the health crisis, but their challenges fell on deaf ears. Any suggestion of wrongdoing was flatly denied, even ridiculed, and popular media perpetuated the mockery.

*   *   *

Terry was managing her condition at home. She wasn't considered to be severe or contagious. She flicked on the TV just in time to catch a news report: "The World Bank has downgraded the British government's financial rating. The national debt is now so high, it's expected that the UK will be placed in Special Measures as our repayment plan is reviewed. The spiralling cost of statutory sick pay, incapacity benefit and disability benefits is bankrupting the country. And it's not looking like this situation will change in the forseeable future. The impact of disease is expected to condemn the world economy to a deep and lasting recession.

"Welfare cuts across Europe have resulted in mass protests, but government officials are saying they have no choice. The only businesses thriving are the health sectors - pharmaceuticals, doctors, alternative therapies, and private healthcare. People are willing to spend all their savings on anything that might offer a cure, or even relieve their symptoms.

"Francesca from the lobby group 'Stop the Disease' is with us. What are your members saying?" asked the reporter.

"People are furious!" said Francesca. "The British government has managed this appallingly. Quarantine for the worst affected was too late and ineffective. Their failure to deliver a vaccine or a cure has caused mass panic, resulting in many unnecessary deaths, and we're totally outraged."

"Have other countries done any better?"

"In some countries, earlier quarantine slowed down the spread of the disease. And that's important when there's no cure!" She was fuming.

*   *   *

The most alarming news was when increasing numbers of younger people with no underlying conditions started to die in hospitals and treatment centres. The virulence of disease seemed to be increasing, forcing people to make tough choices and separate themselves from their loved ones if they became sick. Some were desperate to protect the children. Others started to self-isolate and avoid human contact altogether. People stayed away from public events and stopped going out. Businesses closed. People were frightened, staying home, yet the disease continued to spread.

The treatment centres set up by the military to take pressure off the hospitals were now full to capacity. Make-shift morgues were set up to process the dead. World economies sank into recession and welfare was cut to stop the government from going bankrupt.

Unable to rely on welfare, people were forced back to work wherever they could find it, but substantial numbers were unwell and exhausted - not functioning at their best. The government's position was that in an emergency situation, everyone had to pull their weight. Meanwhile, in the workplace, there was rising concern about whether the people who were ill might infect others around them. Social distancing measures were put in place, but with limited effectiveness.

The media started calling the disease 'the new plague'. Small teams of skeleton staff kept the papers, radio and TV news running. Everyone wanted to know the latest news, but in many sectors of the economy, people had been laid off, were struggling to find work, pay the rent, and feed themselves.

Panic buying, workforce sickness, and severe economic recession led to food shortages and people losing their homes. Churches and charities opened their doors, allowing those who'd lost everything to have warmth and shelter for the night, but they were struggling too.

Spiralling interest rates forced governments to borrow and raise taxes, leaving people who were still working poorer, while working twice as hard to cover for absent colleagues. Workers took to the streets in protest, and unions called for their members to strike.

"Government out!" they chanted, as they thronged outside Westminster, shouting angrily at any passing MP, held back by riot police. Half the politicians were off sick too.

Across the country people tuned in to hear the latest news. Terry's friend Charlotte thought the newsreader on ITV didn't look particularly well. "The specialist treatment centres holding the most diseased people outside the city are now full to capacity, and critics are arguing that they're ineffective. The disease continues to spread and worsen at great haste in our towns and cities. It looks like the government has lost the battle and there are no real solutions being put forward. Some people respond positively to creams and medication, some respond to anti-allergy treatments, but there's no cure in sight, and the exact cause of the disease remains a mystery. The only theory proposed was by Dr David Leeman who said he believes it's caused by a fungal mutation, but his theory was dismissed some months ago, leaving officials with nowhere to turn. He didn't come up with a cure.

"This week, the government will introduce emergency food rationing, as farmers report manpower problems and low productivity, resulting in severe food shortages. Imports have fallen, reflecting similar problems overseas. This crisis is getting deeper with every passing day, but there's no one from government departments available to comment. Just a statement..."

The camera cut to a film of the Prime Minister. "We have our top people working on a cure. There's no need for panic. If you fear you might be contagious, stay indoors. More specialist treatment centres will be opening soon, offering the best medical treatments to those with the most severe cases of disease. We will publish updates as they become available."

Back to the newsreader. "One thing that has been noted is that in poorer countries the disease is much less prevalent. There are far fewer cases, and they're generally contained."

The phone rang. "Have you seen the news?" said Terry.

"Yes!" said Charlotte, "And I'm seriously considering going to stay with my friend in Morocco! I've managed to avoid this disease so far, but for how long? This is terrifying!"

"Sounds like a good idea," said Terry.

"Too right. People are dying. The whole situation's awful!'"

"When would you come back?"

"I don't know. I wouldn't want to outstay my welcome. But it would be good to escape until it's safe to come back to the UK."

"Do you think you'll be able to get a flight?"

"I hope so, there are a few still departing. I'd need to check."

"One thing I don't understand is why I've had skin problems for a long time," Terry looked at her arm, and screwed up her nose, "but others are getting worse symptoms and dying!"

"Maybe it's not the same thing."

"The dermatologist seems to think it is."

"Well yours seems to be under control."

"I wish."

"They don't seem to think you're contagious."

"No, It's annoying, but it's nothing like as bad as some people's experiences."

"Just as well. I guess some people have more natural resistance than others. I think a lot of people are frightened of being carted away against their will. They're keeping their heads down and hoping no one notices they've got symptoms."

"Probably. I'd hate to end up in one of those specialist treatment centres. I'd be afraid I'd never get out alive."

"Me too."

Charlotte managed to book a flight and paid an extended visit to her friend in the quiet seaside town of Ksar es Seghir, Morocco, while the developed world went into economic meltdown.

Everything was happening so fast. A week later Terry heard that the country's medical facilities were being expanded. "New specialist treatment centres are opening across the country," reported the BBC, "but sheer numbers mean there is a risk of people falling through the net. Places in the centres are limited, but there are good facilities for those who most need them. People who are badly diseased can admit themselves, but if they prefer to stay at home, they are advised to avoid contact with other people."

In rural locations, former workhouses, halls, conference centres and barns were used to house patients suffering from the worst of the outbreak. Huge tents housed additional make-shift wards, where the disease could be contained.

Yet still it spread in towns and cities – children had been coming home from school with white speckles on their skin and the beginnings of an infection, so the schools were closed, but it was hard to keep them apart from their friends. Parents hid them away, afraid of their children being taken to treatment centres by the military. They weren't considered contagious, but people were becoming paranoid. "Better to be safe than sorry".

Support networks were set up, both among the sick and the healthy, to handle the situation. There an increasing prevalence of diseased people being told to leave their homes by frightened loved ones, just trying to protect the rest of their family. Others left voluntarily, to save those they loved from becoming ill. Some went direct to hospitals or treatment centres, but not all of them were ill enough to be admitted.

There were signs of animals becoming infected, with fur falling out and bare patches appearing on people's pets and livestock. The military started shooting and disposing of infected animals. Personnel wore special suits, so they didn't come into direct contact with diseased pets or livestock. Yet still, the infection spread.

*   *   *

The Skype jingle jangled and Charlotte picked up the call.

"Hello mate!" Terry was grinning back at her. "How's it going in Morocco?"

"OK! A lot less illness here," replied Charlotte.

"Glad you went?"

"I think so. It's good to have a change of scenery. I'm enjoying the sea views and the sunshine. It's cheap living and nice to catch up with people I haven't seen in a long time. You?"

"I'm OK. It sounds lovely out there! I'm starting to wonder if David Leeman's fungi theory of disease is right. I've been reading about it. Some of the lobby groups who support him are getting noticed. The natural health community recognised the signs of fungal infection from the outset, apparently."

"But those theories were disproved."

"Dismissed rather than disproved I think. It wouldn't be the first time someone's been ridiculed only to turn out to be right, would it?"

"I guess not."

"Holistic therapists are doing a good trade, and some people swear their approaches are helpful. They have their own tests, but as far as I know, the symptoms can only be managed. There's no cure."

"Have you tried anything new?"

"No. I was just wondering if I should. I've been reading about it. Some people found a short-term benefit from using antifungal drugs, but then they stopped working and the condition got worse again. Apparently that's a common problem."

"It's a dilemma, I know. It'd be easy to spend your life savings on private medical consultations or holistic therapies and be no better at the end of it."

"Yes. Been there. Done that. So tell me more about Morocco!"
They chatted for a while.

Chapter 30
Desperation

As time passed, the government's team of researchers found better ways to manage the condition, but they were unable to cure it. Some people were able to treat the symptoms and continue with their lives, but others continued to decline. The disease became more virulent with time, overwhelming people's immune systems. This made it more deadly, wiping out whole populations in a relatively short period of time.

Deaths were recorded in their millions across the globe. The situation was completely out of control. Hospitals were overwhelmed with many staff taken ill. The military were suffering huge losses. No group was immune.

A general election was due to take place in the UK, but after the leader of the main opposition party fell ill and died, Members of Parliament in the House of Commons voted to form an emergency government, representing all parties. MPs realised that there simply weren't the staff available to hold an election or count the ballots. Too many people were ill. People were just trying to survive. Ministers worked cooperatively across different parties, combining ideas and resources to fight the disease and get society back on its feet.

Leeman published his fungi theory of disease in a series of online articles, opening up new debates about the best approach to tackling the disease. Signs of the disease started to show on his skin - it was superficial and not particularly bothersome, but he knew how this panned out if he didn't find a way to stop its progression. Supportive activists help spread his message through social media - they were keen to support him in any way they could.

Three schools of thought were developing:

Firstly, the doomsday scenario, where mankind was experiencing the end of the world, and there was nothing that could be done. Some said it must be God's bidding.

Secondly, the humanist scenario, where people had complete faith in mankind's ingenuity to find a medical cure through conventional approaches to drug development, even if the process was long winded and painful.

And finally, the natural approach, where society's misfits, weirdos, and hippies sought non-intrusive, holistic approaches to healing. Broadly speaking, they believed it was the 21st century chemically-loaded, medicated, stressful lifestyle that was at fault.

Leeman was finding some common ground with this third group, having seen the devastating error of his ways in pharmaceuticals. People still listening to government propaganda hadn't realised his new generation drugs were largely to blame for the outbreak of disease.

Online support groups exploded in number as people shared their woes, successes, ideas and theories for managing the disease. Beneficial lifestyles with reduced symptoms were trending, and new ideas for managing the condition seeped through the gloom into the collective consciousness. Clean eating and eliminating toxic and manmade chemicals were popular, but making lifestyle changes in a disease ridden world wasn't easy. It wasn't a good time to be choosy about what you ate.

With so much illness, there were food shortages, because farm workers and crop pickers were in short supply. Seasonal workers from other countries stayed away because the disease was less prevalent at home. Flights were mostly cancelled anyway, and many regulars weren't well enough to work.

Farmers resorted to 'pick your own' signs, to get the crops out into the communities. Availability in stores was erratic with some parts of the country well supplied and others experiencing shortages and delays.

Small groups of young healthy individuals took to the remote countryside to avoid contagion in the towns and cities. They would live a self-sufficient natural lifestyle, and some believed this helped keep them healthy.

*   *   *

Terry was feeling alone and afraid. Her disease seemed to have worsened again, giving her skin a nasty patchy appearance. The sores were tender to touch.

"They're still saying it might be an allergic reaction to something in my environment," she said to Charlotte on a call.

"But they don't know what you're allergic to?"

"No. And its hard to get an appointment with a specialist these days. They're overwhelmed."

"Not good. Are you sure it's not a resurgence of your old problem?"

"No. This is different. The white patchy skin and lesions. It's the new disease, all right. Unfortunately. The treatment that resolved my previous problem makes this one worse. It's driving me crazy. Itchy and uncomfortable. I'm knackered all the time and I've started to get the other symptoms. Now I feel bloated and dizzy too. They said it's probably all related, but with no clue what's causing it, I just feel helpless. You did the right thing moving away!"

"It's more common here than it used to be," said Charlotte. "Have they given you anything to manage the symptoms?"

"I've got prescribed steroids and some topical creams to soothe my skin, but they only go so far. They're not working as well as they used to either. I'd like to get out and be more active, but I don't feel up to it. I miss feeling good! I so hope someone gets to the bottom of this soon."

*   *   *

Many people felt hopeless as the world they knew changed beyond recognition. Suicide rates went up. Hospitals were overwhelmed. Economic collapse meant getting basics could be challenging. As the sickness took over much of the developed world, people were starting to lose hope.

Is this it? Terry sat in her bed, contemplating the future of human existence. *I'm so weary. I must've been asleep for 12 hours. I'm exhausted. Limbs like lead weights. I need more energy. How? How can I reduce the bloating, think more clearly? Soothe the discomfort? Feel more normal?*

This had gone way beyond cosmetic irritations – her skin had become tender and painful in places. She didn't feel at all well. *A bit sick actually. What on earth do I do now? The medical profession are under-resourced, overstretched, and don't seem to be able to offer any hope.* She started fervently exploring alternatives to medicine.

Survival in the village was becoming more difficult. Terry's employer had closed the shop because he'd become ill and couldn't continue. Terry was living on savings - couldn't seem to get a response from the welfare office. Now she had to drive to town to get groceries, and half the time the shops were shut there too, due to staff shortages and supply problems. People were stock-piling so you had to take whatever you could get.

What do I do when the money runs out? she pondered. *People are saying benefits have been cut, claims are being turned down. I can't even get through. I need to improve my health, so I can work... if only there were enough jobs to go around. This is truly horrendous.*

In the early days of Smooth's introduction, she'd followed David Leeman's work with great curiosity, elevating him to god-like status when he won the Nobel Prize.

Scrolling through Google she found dozens of articles about Leeman - some praising his work, some ridiculing his ideas, some about his expulsion from the government research committee. *I'm amazed someone can fall so far from grace! How did he end up flying the flag for the natural health community?*

She read Leeman's latest published works - his highly controversial and widely dismissed idea that this disease could be caused by a fungus. *It kind-of makes sense to me,* she thought. *I'm no expert... But what if he's right?*

Medical professionals had dismissed his work as mumbo jumbo, using 'unproven techniques' and 'fanciful ideas'. These were the same medical professionals who didn't have a clue how to treat the disease. *Could it be true that the best approach is to treat it like a fungus?*

She decided to give it a try and made some lifestyle changes. 'Fungi thrive on blood sugar, so try to avoid peaks in your blood sugar levels. This is good for your overall health too,' suggested one of the articles. She decided to cut out sweet foods and switched to consuming mostly low-carbohydrate foods such as green vegetables and protein-rich foods. 'It's a good idea to avoid all antibacterial products and medicines, and avoid all fungi'. She tossed her remaining tube of Smooth into the back of the drawer.

She wasn't ready to bin it, but it only seemed to make the symptoms worse. 'Do not use recreational drugs' - well that seemed obvious and was illegal anyway. She resolved not to use Kayl. 'Drink only plain filtered water'. She ordered a water filter online. It was just as well some companies were still trading. The rules went on and on, with some seeming rather neurotic. There was a list of natural antifungals at the end, which included raw garlic and herbal extracts. She selected a couple that were inexpensive and easy to obtain.

As weeks passed, Terry found her new regime helped a little. Her symptoms reduced in severity. Her skin condition improved and the sores settled down. She was no longer in pain. *Perhaps there is something in Leeman's theory after all.*

* * *

Stephen's disease had spread and he'd fallen into a deep depression. "I've never exactly fitted into society, but now I'm a social pariah!" he complained to Mark.

"Join the club mate!" High on *hot caffeine*, as usual.

"All I ever wanted was to be loved and respected, just for being me, but apparently that's expecting too much." He huffed and fidgeted. "My whole life, everyone has always wanted me to change, to be something different, to be someone that I'm not - and can never be."

"They're bastards mate, the lot of them."

"I tried to conform! I tried wearing what other people wear and doing what other people do, but they were still nasty and ridiculed me. So I gave up."

"Too right. Forget about them. Don't let the bastards get you down."

"I thought I'd finally found a group of people who accepted me, but now I've got this horrible disease, it's like being back at square one. This thing has spread to other parts of my body. It's making me feel weird. Woozy. I don't blame my old buddies for not wanting to catch it, but half of them are showing signs of disease too."

"Think I've got it mate. Affecting everyone. The woozy thing's not so bad. You just need to chill. Hey, have some *hot caffeine*. It helps."

Stephen was really struggling. Not wanting to blot out his misery with drugs, but unsure how else to cope. He'd given up seeking thrills or approval, and was now more interested in finding a cure. Like Terry, he'd heard about Leeman's work. The way the scientist had bombed from being a respected genius, to being completely discredited, appealed to his own sense of alienation. The press had dragged Leeman's name through the mud with a great sense of glee. Some suggested he'd lost his mind. Stephen sympathised, having felt total rejection from society himself.

Even if Leeman's right, there's no immediate cure, and little likelihood of finding one, he thought, *but I'd like to be involved in any trials.*

Chapter 31
New Hope

Some American health clinics had, for years, been endeavouring to cure all manner of disease by harnessing the power of the body's own immune system, rather than by suppressing the symptoms with drugs. It was a model Leeman supported, but it was very controversial, with variable outcomes and little scientific evidence to back up the good results.

Fortunately, a generous benefactor, Abraham, who was also experiencing early signs of the disease, saw potential in Leeman's work and offered to provide funding for a new treatment facility. This wealthy businessman had seen his fortunes slide as economic woes faced the western world, but with what was left, he wanted to do something to help people and improve the situation.

He arranged to meet David Leeman. "It's a travesty that this epidemic has got so out of control," said the businessman. "I feel completely disillusioned by the medical profession. They insist there's nothing wrong with me, and the so-called government is completely incompetent. I've been following your work with a keen interest, and I'd like to work with you to fund and develop a new research and treatment facility. Are you open to the idea?"

"Yes! Absolutely!" Leeman didn't need to be asked twice.

"Good. You should never have been dismissed from the government research committee and I'd like to make things right. Will you run the new centre for me?"

"I'd love to!" He grinned from ear to ear.

"Excellent. I envisage our mission will be to power-up the immune system to fight the disease. It will be a commune for those seeking wellness through natural means, although if you come up with a pharmaceutical solution to all our woes, we certainly won't rule it out!"

"OK. Sounds good. So who do we take with us?"

"People affected by the disease are welcome to apply for membership, but they'll have to commit to our strict healthy lifestyle, treatment regime, and abide by our rules on appropriate behaviours. The environment inside the commune will be controlled, and people's progress will be monitored. We'll do everything we can to eradicate this disease, regardless of what is happening in the outside world. Are you in?"

"Yes!" said Leeman excitedly, "I can't wait to get started."

A large derelict boarding school, parts of which had been reclaimed by nature, provided the perfect location for the isolated commune. It was hidden away in the Chiltern Hills, away from population hubs, and was adjacent to abandoned agricultural land that offered the opportunity for self-sufficiency. Abandoned buildings, knocked into shape, could house people living in the commune. The key thing was that everyone there must buy into the philosophy of the project.

As the old boarding school buildings were acquired and improved, word spread about the new healing centre and the wacky community that was about to move into them. Traditional media - which had mostly moved online now - ridiculed the concept, labelling Abraham and David Leeman as deluded loonies. They ran cartoon strips making fun of the twosome. But their readers were dropping like flies.

A website was set up, explaining the nature of the project: "The commune's philosophy is to strive for optimal health, based on clean, natural living. It will be a research centre, run by David Leeman, studying ways to enhance the power of the immune system. Those living at the centre can volunteer to test anything new that's developed as part of the programme."

There was no room for sceptics of the natural health movement here. Sceptics considered it a place where weirdos and the deluded went to die.

"You must be able to demonstrate a commitment to our shared values and vision," explained the website. "We don't want people who are going to cause angst, disagreements and disharmony. A stress-free lifestyle and a supportive environment are key to the whole concept."

As word spread, hundreds of desperate people applied to join the commune. Each offered what they could in terms of practical help or financial assistance. The buildings were vast, with many dormitories, so most applications were accepted.

Terry was among the first to apply. "I'd love to join!" she said, brimming with enthusiasm at her entry interview. "I've come as far as I can on my own. I'm open to the idea that this condition is caused by a fungus. My symptoms have improved a lot on an antifungal health regime. I've learnt to manage the symptoms on my own, but I want a cure. I'm keen to try new things to boost my immunity."

Leeman looked her up and down. She had the disease badly, but it did look like some of her sores were healing. "You've done well to find a way of managing it," he said. "You do realise we haven't developed any kind of cure at the moment? We're staying as close to nature as we can get, and we want to harness the power of the immune system by supporting it with beneficial foods, changed lifestyles, natural herbs and medicinal plants. If we do develop a drug to assist recovery, it too, will be as close to nature as possible."

Terry nodded. "Yes, I understand," she said. "Modern medicine seems to have little to offer me, so as far as I'm concerned, this is the way to go."

"We'll all follow a strict programme of healthy living and detoxification," he continued. "This is a crucial part of the process. You'll undoubtedly find some of our methods strange - they've been laughed at by the medical profession for years, but they're all in place for good reasons."

Terry smiled - still keen.

"We'll be living a clean purifying life," Leeman continued, "eliminating toxic chemicals from our lives and working to clean up our bodies, so that our immune systems can function more effectively. Outside of the commune, most people think we're mad."

Terry was entranced by the concept. "I completely understand and that sounds perfect. I was always a believer in natural approaches to healing, and only defected to pharmaceutical drugs because I was desperate. Working with the body's natural defences is much more aligned to my beliefs. Please let me join the commune. I'll be an asset, not a bore."

Leeman smiled warmly, "OK, you're in. We open in a couple of weeks, so if you turn up at the commune on opening day, we'll find you a bed. It helps us very much if you can contribute in funds or in practical ways, as we have limited resources."

"Of course – that goes without saying. I'll help in any way I can," she nodded.

The opening day was very busy and there was an air of excitement and anticipation. Those moving in had many shared values and beliefs. It was an exhilarating place to be. They exchanged ideas, optimism and lived a healthy way of life. Detached from the doom and gloom eclipsing the rest of the world, this seemed like the most positive place to be. The commune, and those staying within it, came to be known as the Freedom Seekers.

* * *

Alex was inspired by the movement - if a bit conflicted because Leeman, his arch enemy, was running the commune. But the scientist seemed to have switched sides and was now working with the natural health lobby, which he had to concede, was a good thing. *If he's seen the light and admitted the error of his ways, that's good. Although I hate how he manipulated Terry.*

Alex longed for a community where his beliefs were shared and valued, where animal cruelty was despised and natural methods of healing were embraced. *I wonder if they'd let me join the Freedom Seekers,* he pondered, *when I'm free from this wretched institution. I know a lot about natural health. I could be an asset.*

Alex and Jessica devised ways to see more of each other at Newfield Psychiatric Clinic. They became close. Jessica confided in him. "My skin problem has spread, but the doctors say I'm worrying too much... their tests show everything is 'normal', which means I have to live with it. They say it won't kill me. Might be a mild allergy, they said," She revealed some patchy skin on her midriff and didn't look impressed. "Do you think this looks normal?" she asked. "Honestly?"

He shook his head, "No, not at all. They just don't know what's wrong with you, so they say everything's normal. They won't admit their own ignorance or acknowledge their own limitations. Anyone can see there's something physically wrong, but they just don't know what it is, so they say it's normal. Keratin overgrowth has become normal. Allergies are now normal. But they can never say what people are allergic to. It's a joke."

She looked sad.

"Hey," he said kindly, "Come here." He reached out, took her in his arms and gave her a hug, "You know what we're gonna do when we get out of here?" She shook her head - *not a clue*.

"We're going to get well naturally," he announced with absolute certainty, looking at the white spots on his own arm, "and we're going to do it without cruelty or drugs." He'd found a new soul mate, and her name was Jessica.

Chapter 32
Theories of a Madman

The government was at a loss.

"No one's coming up with any answers!" said the Prime Minister to his dwindling cabinet. "We've got millions of people infected with what the media are calling 'the plague', but no effective treatment. Our scientific committee is worse than useless and the medical profession is perplexed.

"People are dying in their millions across the globe and we're scratching our heads! It's not good enough. The NHS is on its knees, hospitals have closed their doors to new patients, due to staff shortages and lack of capacity, and the worldwide economy is in meltdown. What happened to the man… what's his name… Leeman - who showed such promise?"

An MP shifted in his chair uncomfortably, "They brought him in to help with the research but he started developing wacko theories. Everyone thought he'd lost his mind so he was dismissed from the project. He was just getting in the way Sir. We didn't want people without any credibility on the team. We've got the best minds working on it now."

"But they're not producing any results - nothing satisfactory anyway. We're not moving forward. Why were Leeman's theories 'wacko'?"

"He had this silly idea that the disease was caused by a fungal infection Sir. It's been a long standing idea, perpetuated by radical doctors for decades, that fungi can cause major disease in otherwise healthy people, but the theories have been disproved so many times. Some people just won't let it go."

"What if Dr Leeman is right?"

"He isn't sir. They've done tests, looked into it. He's just deluded. He's not the first. There was an Italian doctor, Dr Tullio Simoncini who back in 2005, wrote a book about his theory that cancer was a fungus - his ideas were ridiculed and dismissed, and he was struck off the medical register. His reputation never recovered. He started working in the natural health sector, trying to cure people from cancer by injecting them with bicarbonate of soda! Of all the ridiculous ideas! One of his patients died and he got a five year jail term in 2018."

"OK. But that's not the same thing that we're dealing with now."

"No, but Dr Leeman has been discredited too, after declaring that his tests showed the current epidemic of disease was caused by a fungus. He's using technology that no one else is familiar with, and getting results that no one else believes in. People think his wife's death made him mad and I'm afraid he's become the butt of many medical jokes in recent times."

Upon hearing all this, the Prime Minister had a rather different idea. "Hmmm. If all these so called 'experts' can't come up with anything, I want to bring this radical scientist back into our fold and hear what he has to say. I think there could be a chance that he's right. I want to hear his theories for myself and we'll take it from there."

*   *   *

Leeman was brought before the Prime Minister to explain his theory.

"It's very simple sir. I've developed technology that enables me to identify the fungus by its DNA. It goes beyond traditional DNA sequencing, so the results are clearer and easier to interpret. The technology is very new, but as far as I am concerned, it's fully developed and I have complete faith in it. I believe my results to be 100% accurate and correct. I will be studying the fungus further within the Freedom Seekers commune, and hope to develop new treatments, as presently, it is resistant to all existing antifungal drugs.

"At the moment, we're working to boost the immune system," he continued, "through lifestyle interventions and natural approaches to healthcare. Time will tell just how much we can do to help people suffering from this dreadful disease."

A prolonged discussion ensued and Leeman left, having given the Prime Minister plenty to think about.

"I think this man's research is in the public interest," said the Prime Minister, after due consideration. "To dismiss his results just because the technology is new and flies in the face of conventional wisdom, does not mean his results are incorrect. It might just be that he's one step ahead of the rest of the scientific fraternity – and it wouldn't be the first time that one outstanding individual has left his peers behind. This health crisis is too big and too devastating to ignore his theories. Give him whatever he needs to conduct these studies properly."

Despite economic meltdown and the welfare system crumbling under sick claims, the government poured everything they could into Leeman's research over the next six months, while Abraham managed the community, freeing the scientist up to spend his time in the lab.

Leeman was granted access to the best laboratory facilities in the country and given a new government-funded research team who believed in his work. He travelled between the Freedom Seekers HQ and the lab in Oxford, where much of the research was taking place.

Meanwhile, the Freedom Seekers were following a strict protocol, with new people joining the commune every day. They combined different approaches to detoxify, boost immunity, and improve their health. The regime included a raw vegan diet, daily saunas, organic food, and purified water. No manmade chemicals were allowed on site, unless under strict authorisation. Vinegar and lemon were used for cleaning. Everything in the facility was natural. Green juices, wheatgrass, and immune-boosting foods were consumed regularly and there was no wifi or mobile phone use allowed on site due to the risk of negative health effects. All technologies were plugged in.

"Hey, good to see you guys," said Terry when she met new recruits, Kevin and Mark in the corridor. "Coming to yoga?"

"Yeah!" said Mark. "Love yoga - feel really chilled afterwards."

Kev grinned and gave her a thumbs up. "We'll see you there."

In the afternoons they took gentle exercise, infrared saunas, and helped out with work projects in the commune. Some people struggled with the exercise, especially if they had chronic fatigue, but everyone pushed themselves to do what they could. Members took part in immune therapies, oxygen treatment, music, massage, even laughter therapy. Everyone had a role to play and contributed to the community lifestyle.

"Don't forget your nutritional supplements!" said Terry as she waved goodbye to the lads.

They waved back and grinned.

These combined efforts helped to harness the power of people's immune systems, reducing symptoms and the effects of disease.

Outside, most people still dismissed the centre as ludicrous. The mainstream press ran cartoons making fun of the facility, but others saw it as their only hope.

One day Alex and Jessica realised that staff shortages at the clinic were so bad, that security was lax.

"Alex, there's no one in reception!" said Jess and she peered into the foyer.

"Really? Can you grab the keys?" he said.

They walked free from the 'secure' hospital and clinic unaided, simply by stealing the keys from the abandoned reception desk. The staff were so stretched that no one cared any more. The couple made their way to the Freedom Seekers facility. Word on the street - and the wards - was that if you wanted to live, it was probably your best hope.

They passed bodies decaying in the streets, people wailing, scenes of utter devastation. "Oh crikes, I think it was better inside!" said Jess.

*   *   *

In the Oxford lab, a team meeting was in full swing. "We need to look at all possible solutions," said Leeman. "We mustn't rule anything out. I've got volunteers back at the commune willing to test synthetic interferons to boost the immune system, oxygen treatments, plant compounds, antifungal oil extracts, experimental nanotechnology, and anything else that might show promise. If you have ideas, I want to hear them all."

The trials were greeted with great hope and optimism, but nothing seemed to have a consistent and lasting benefit. The research team gained a better understanding of how the fungi resisted intervention, how it mutated and evolved, but progress was slow.

An opportunity came up to trial a veterinary drug called lufenuron. "Count me in," said Terry.

"OK, this drug was developed to kill fleas on cats and dogs," Leeman explained, "but it has antifungal properties too. It was never licensed for human use, probably because it does carry

141

some risk, including digestive disturbances and nausea, but the risks of short term use are thought to be low. High doses may be riskier. Right now, we're looking at low doses, and you can stop at any time. Are you sure you're happy to proceed?"

"Yes," said Terry. "I've read about it. Been around for ages and some people online swear it's good against fungal infections. So I'm keen to give it a go." She was one of 12 who'd agreed to testing the drug, and there was a chorus of agreement among the others.

Leeman began trials. After a couple of weeks, most participants were delighted. "Wow, this stuff's good!" he said, as people saw rapid improvement. But after a promising couple of weeks, it simply stopped working.

"Oh no," said Leeman. "The fungus has developed resistance. That's so disappointing."

A second study group tried it, and the same thing happened. They were getting nowhere. Leeman and his team pursued other avenues, starting development of a promising immunotherapy drug, but it faltered at the first hurdle when it turned out to be toxic. Within six months the government funding had dried up. Abraham funded smaller projects within the commune, and they continued working towards better health naturally.

"Today, we have grave news," reported BBC Radio 4, now on skeleton staff and occasionally broadcasting updates. "The British government has been declared bankrupt and government officials who still have their health have moved underground for their own protection. State spending has been stopped. Any taxes taken will go towards paying back government debts. Financially, and in many other respects, the people of Britain are on their own."

As the government fell and the economy collapsed, it really was survival of the fittest. Everyone for themselves.

Within the commune, the infection was under control. People weren't dying and the fungus wasn't spreading the way it did in the outside world. People's infections weren't getting worse. Some saw slow improvements on the Freedom Seekers' regime. They were pinning their hopes on Leeman coming up with a miracle.

One of the things that was still hard to ignore, was that the disease was less prolific in parts of the developing world, where the new generation of antibiotics had typically been less available to the masses, or less affordable. And where Kayl was less inclined to grow. Some westerners had moved to lesser-developed countries, to try and escape 'the plague', but as people with infections moved overseas in search of wellness, they spread the disease across the developing world too.

Chapter 33
Devastation

The commune, located in an isolated part of the Chilterns countryside, had become a bubble of relative wellness, sheltering people from the outside world and keeping them in good shape, so their symptoms didn't get worse. Members learnt to live with their conditions, embracing healthy lifestyles, organic growing, relaxation techniques, and mutual support. A peaceful and positive lifestyle helped keep their stress levels down, their immunity optimised, and the symptoms of disease at bay.

The Freedom Seekers project was considered to be a success, not because they'd found a cure for the disease, but because they'd found a way to manage it more successfully than anyone outside. The evasive cure they'd all hoped for at the start? It was still a work in progress. Not forgotten, but perhaps not as urgent as it had seemed when they all moved in.

However, beyond the walls of the commune, the collapse of governments, economies, and societies, had changed everything. The world population dwindled to millions, and there was little hope among those who were left.

In the streets, corpses were cleaned up by carrion, but not fast enough - the stench was awful. Survivors were steering clear of the cities, except for when they went scavenging for supplies. Authority had long ceased to exist and there was no power, unless you generated it yourself. Solar panels and small wind turbines kept everything ticking along inside the commune. The Freedom Seekers lived happily inside their fenced-off compound, protected from the horrors of the outside world.

Within months of government collapse, all official channels of communication had ceased. Occasional radio broadcasts from survivors could be heard, but there was little else in the way of contact with the wider world. A natural water supply near the base was found, ready for when the taps ran dry. Treatment and filtration systems were put in place to ensure it was safe to drink.

Food supplies were more challenging, because during cold weather little would grow. Supplies of the nutritionally dense foods that members needed to optimise their immune systems and promote healing, were increasingly unavailable. Reluctantly, they were forced to compromise the regime.

Connections were made with surviving farmers but they were struggling too, and had a limited supply of produce. They'd lost their labourers and were living self-sufficiently in small family groups. Growing food crops without agricultural chemicals was hard. Life was becoming increasingly perilous as everything the western world took for granted fell away.

The Freedom Seekers tried to grow more produce within the grounds of the commune. They'd already expanded their community farm into nearby fields. But as society fell apart, anyone left in the outside world was playing a game of survival - theft was rife and security, troublesome. The Freedom Seekers became as self-sufficient as they could, but the people were many, and the crops were slow to grow. The challenges seemed overwhelming. The group pulled together - everyone had valuable roles to play. Some worked in farming, others in the kitchens, some as therapists, in maintenance, in cleaning, security, admissions and gate management. The commune was a well-oiled machine. Everyone did their bit and that's why it worked.

Chapter 34
New Arrivals

Jessica and Alex reached the Freedom Seekers, buzzed the intercom at the gate, and begged the warden to let them join the commune. He took them inside and went through the usual questions.

"We've travelled a long way and have read all about your methods," said Jessica. "It's fascinating. We're keen to get involved and are completely committed to following the regime. We're hard workers and can contribute in many ways to community life."

Alex was quiet - he let Jessica do the talking. After a prolonged exchange, the warden checked his records and said, "OK. You seem to meet the admissions criteria. We're almost full, but I am authorised to let you in on a trial basis." He found them each a bed in the dorms.

The following morning, Terry went to meditation class and spotted Alex across the hall, eyes shut, looking deeply relaxed and enjoying the peacefulness of the moment.

She went straight to find Leeman. "I need a word urgently!" she said.

"What's up? Is everything OK?"

"There's a new member in the meditation hall and I know him."

"Is that a problem?"

"Yes! It's Alex!" She looked at him tentatively. "The man who murdered your wife."

Leeman's expression turned from confusion to alarm. "That monster?" he said. "He's here?"

Leeman choked back the anger and the tears as he struggled to contain his emotions. "He has to go!" he said.

He picked up the phone. "Security? We have a convicted murderer in our midst and he needs to be removed. Get the whole security team together and meet me outside the main hall where morning meditation is taking place."

Terry was worried. "He's dangerous," she said. "He was locked up in an institution and must have escaped. He frightens me. How did he even get in here?"

Leeman was visibly shaking, "The wardens wouldn't necessarily recognise him."

At the main hall, Leeman identified Alex and three burly security men went to remove him.

"You can't stay here. Letting you in was a mistake," Leeman said coldly. "We can't have murderers and arsonists in our midst – and I personally can't be in the same place as you. Now leave."

"I've changed!" he pleaded, "Let me stay!" His eyes were begging, desperate, full of regret.

"I don't care how much you've changed," said Leeman. "You murdered my wife and destroyed my life. You've terrorised Terry. There may be no authorities to arrest and contain you any more, but that doesn't mean we have to take responsibility for you. You're on your own."

"I can't survive on my own!" he protested. "I've always been a supporter of natural health. This facility is my dream. Don't you understand?"

"No. Get out of here," said Leeman coldly.

"I was angry!" he shouted as he was dragged away. "You were torturing innocent animals, involving Terry in clinical trials! Now I'm on your side. I've learnt compassion. I've worked on my anger issues. I want a normal life. Let me prove I've changed!"

"Never," said Leeman, who turned his back and left. Alex was taken to the gates and escorted outside by the three security men.

When Jessica found out she was gutted.

*   *   *

Stephen was ill, tired and felt like giving up, but there was a spark within him that wanted to keep fighting. He'd heard about the Freedom Seekers on TV and radio, before communications had died. Mark and Kevin had decided to go there, but he didn't want to at the time. The whole set-up had been mercilessly ridiculed and became the butt of many jokes - he didn't think it would last five minutes.

147

People said they were the deluded followers of a mad scientist who'd lost his mind when his wife was murdered. But as the disease wiped out billions of people across the globe, and the Freedom Seekers survived, even thrived, it didn't really matter what anyone else thought.

I wonder if I can make it to the facility. Should've gone with Mark and Kevin. Does it still exist? I guess I can travel there - try to find it. The roads were treacherous - there were gangs on every corner wanting to steal supplies. Not that Stephen had many supplies. It was a dangerous environment for anyone on their own, and as usual, Stephen was on his own.

He was approached by a gang almost as soon as he tried to leave London. "Give us your food and water and we'll leave you be!" they demanded, pointing guns at his car. This wasn't the time to argue. He opened the car door to offer them his groceries, but they took a closer look at his face, and said, "Urgh, he's diseased! Keep moving! We don't want food from his kind!" So he carried on his way.

He arrived at the Freedom Seekers facility inside an old boarding school, in a rural part of the Chilterns. It was quiet and looked like a prison or a high-security military base. The eight foot fencing had barbed wire along the top. He walked around outside feeling anxious and eventually found a locked gate. He called through.

"Hello? Is anyone there?" he stood and waited, then walked a little further around the perimeter. Nothing. It was getting dark.

"Hello?" his call echoed through the emptiness. It seemed hopeless and futile. Perhaps they'd all died too. He wandered a bit further. There were no signs of life. Then the silence was broken by a small female voice.

"Hello. What are you doing out there in the cold?" It was Jessica.

"I want to join the commune. I'll do whatever it takes to get better. Does it still exist?"

"Yes," said Jessica, stepping out of the shadows. "I'll have to go and find our leader, Abraham. No one comes in without his say so these days."

Stephen was relieved. Jessica disappeared and he waited patiently outside. Five minutes later, Abraham appeared alongside her.

"What are your intentions?" he asked Stephen coolly.

"I want to join the wellness programme. I'll do whatever it takes to get better," he said.

"You realise we're a self-sufficient community?"

"Yes," Stephen nodded.

"We expect everyone to do their part, to contribute to the wellbeing of the community, and to stick to our strict regime. No one must endanger the lives of others by doing their own thing and allowing the fungus to spread. We're following some promising leads on our research programme, but it's a long haul, and nothing's going to happen overnight."

"I understand," said Stephen, "Is there space? Can I come in?"

Abraham opened the gate, "It's not luxurious, but there are dormitory spaces still available, and a great supportive community spirit. We're all very much into positive thinking and a holistic approach to healing. You need to think as we do – there is great healing power in a positive disposition. There is no room for anyone who opposes our methods, criticizes our regimes or isn't fully committed to the programme."

He nodded, "I understand, and I'm committed – really I am."

He was welcomed inside.

The following day he met Terry, Jessica, David Leeman, and some of the others on the programme.

"We begin each morning with meditation or yoga," Terry explained, then showed him around the facility – the vegetable gardens, dormitories, canteen, saunas, assembly room and gym. It was such a happy, relaxed atmosphere.

"I'm sure I'll be happy here," he said, "I'm looking forward to the healing activities!" He was filled with a sense of hope and optimism.

Stephen made friends and met Kevin and Mark, who after years of getting high on *hot caffeine*, had become hopelessly infected by the pathogenic fungi, and decided to change their ways.

"Hey man! Great to see you!" said Mark. "You gotta love this place man! It's so cool. Kinda relaxing. When we're not on a work party anyways. Still get to chill. Getting healthier though. Feeling good. Howz you?"

"Hey, good to see you," said Stephen. "Yes, keen to get well. Hoping it works for me."

Mark grinned. "The regime's strict, but it's all good. Makes a lot of sense. The infection was making us miserable, but this regime - well it's working. Kev and I are feeling better for it. Gotta do my meditation, but we'll catch up soon yeah?"

"Definitely."

Mark was certainly more alert and clued up to what was going on than he'd remembered. In their previous life, they were usually high on drugs and spaced out. This was quite a transformation.

*   *   *

Alex was on his own in the city, barely surviving by looting from shops for food and staying in abandoned buildings for shelter. It was a lonely life, the streets were littered with bodies and the whole place stank, but he needed to live in a place where he could find food and supplies. He still suffered from anger management issues, but tried to contain his anger and focus on other things. Anger didn't do him any good and was counter-productive to survival because he was wasting energy with bitter hatred and thoughts of revenge.

He used *hot caffeine* raw from the ground to give him a 'high' and make things seem better than they were. He missed Jessica. Those two had made a real connection, but she was better off in the commune where she stood a chance of wellness.

In the outside world, it was just a waiting game – waiting for death.

Since Alex's departure, Jessica had made friends with Terry and she quickly took a liking to Stephen, enjoying his quirky personality. Mark and Kevin were a bit weird, but they were upbeat and likeable. Jessica's bipolar seemed to be well controlled by the strict health regime at the Freedom Seekers - she was relatively free from depression and from manic episodes, finding herself sharing the optimism and positive vibes of others at the facility. Positivity, it seemed, was contagious.

Chapter 35
Signs of Success

Terry was feeling a lot better. It'd been a year since the Freedom Seekers opened, and she still had symptoms of the disease, but her skin was smoother, less sore, and the digestive problems bothered her less. She'd had sauna therapy, green smoothies and followed the strict health regimes. They weren't always to her liking, but she'd reaped the benefits, and was happy to see the improvement in her health. Many people living outside the commune were in a bad way. Things were getting worse outside. The commune was a lifesaver - literally.

Others in the commune noticed gradual improvements and with each person that showed small signs of getting better, there was new hope.

One of Leeman's old colleagues, Jonathan Melluish, a survivor from the outside, came to visit the Freedom Seekers.

"Wow! A blast from the past!" said Leeman, welcoming the man, who looked grubby and unkempt. It was a stark contrast to the proud man in the pristine white coat that he'd worked with years earlier. Melluish hadn't always supported Leeman's ideas, but he now seemed more open-minded.

"I wanted to connect, because I have knowledge that I think could help you," he explained.

"OK. Sounds good!" said Leeman. "What's on your mind?"

"I don't know if you've seen them," he said, "but there are huge plantations of experimental genetically modified Neem about a mile down the road. The seed was modified to maximise its anti-parasitic and anti-microbial qualities, for possible use in medicine. It's fast growing, and has started to spread into the countryside. I was involved in the early plans, and I think you might find it useful."

"That sounds interesting," said Leeman. "Does it have antifungal properties?"

"I believe so - it was being grown for its wide-ranging antimicrobial benefits. It didn't used to grow in this country, but as the climate's warmed, we've had some success. It's a very hardy strain, able to withstand drought and disease, and has continued growing prolifically without any cultivation from the farmer, who passed away six months ago. There are other plantations around the country, but this one's particularly convenient for you."

"It does sound like something we should investigate."

"Yes, sorry - I should have brought some with me. It's been seeding itself and spreading into the local countryside in recent years, so there are plenty of young bushes around if you can find a use for it. It started growing on hillsides in rural areas - it likes sunny spots. I was looking at its properties and it seems quite potent. I thought it might help your community."

"I'll look into it. Thank you. Now tell me... how are you?"

Leeman looked him up and down. Unkempt, drawn, tired. He could sense an underlying sadness. Despite his positive words, Melluish looked beaten. "In the outside world, we're really struggling," he admitted. "The company's closed. Everything's shut down. That's why I'm no longer investigating the potential of the plant."

"Oh I see. Well why don't you stay with us for a while? We can catch up and exchange ideas. Show me this GM Neem and we can work together again, if you'd like to." Melluish seemed wide open to suggestions, having lost faith in what he thought he knew.

He nodded. "Maybe. You seem to have a good life here."

"It's not bad under the circumstances," Leeman smiled.

The twosome visited the plantation and returned with samples of Neem, then worked together to extract its active compounds, creating a solution with powerful antifungal qualities.

"It looks really promising," said Leeman.

"I told you it had potential!" This was like the old days, working together.

Leeman dropped a spot of it on his arm, where a mild infection festered. Melluish did the same. Leeman went to find Terry, who he knew was keen to try anything.

"Terry – you said you wanted to try anything that looked promising. I have something here," he said.

"Oh – excellent! What is it?"

"A GM Neem extract with antifungal qualities," he replied, "I'd like to put some on your skin and monitor it for the next 24 hours," he said.

"Ooh, not sure about GM," she said. "We used to protest against those trials! Frankenstein foods!"

"OK don't worry. There's no pressure at all. We're just experimenting."

Melluish stayed over and by morning, the two of them had seen a small improvement.

"Wow. That's good," said Leeman. "It seems to be working."

Upon hearing the news, Terry had a change of heart. "OK. I'll try it today," she offered.

Leeman grinned. "Not so principled today, huh?"

Terry smiled back. "Well it's a balance of risk over benefits isn't it. I think the benefits could outweigh the risks on this one..."

Leeman smiled at her change of heart. "OK. I'm just going to drum up some support so we can explore its potential with a larger group."

Leeman went to speak to some other volunteers, keen to replicate the results, and soon a long queue had formed outside the Freedom Seekers' laboratory. Mark and Kevin were keen. Jessica was there. Many people wanted to be a part of the experiment. It was a tentative trial initially, just a drop each - to minimize the chance of any bad reactions.

Terry went first. "Just a drop on the skin," said Leeman. "Let it dry and try not to rub it or wash it off. See how that goes."

"Thank you," she said.

There were no bad reactions, so they continued treatment for a couple of weeks to monitor individual responses, then reviewed the situation. At the review meeting, everyone was excited, because that small area they'd been treating had improved slightly.

"Look! This is so exciting!" said Terry to Stephen. She pointed at her left arm.

"You think that's better?" He wasn't convinced.

"Oh it is. No doubt."

"Well that's promising then. Perhaps I should try it too."

While the development of a cure seemed imminent, ensuring there was enough food to feed everyone was an ongoing challenge. Life was good, but not always easy. A local farmer who'd helped them before, was no longer able to supply fresh food. He had troubles of his own.

The people in the commune tried to grow their own fresh produce and save the seed. Compost toilets provided fertilizer, and sheer persistence and determination enabled the members to grow crops. Outside however, pockets of survivors were existing on whatever they could find, steal, or salvage from derelict shops and buildings. Supermarkets had long been emptied of stock, and every attempt to explore the world outside was plagued with the risk of meeting violent gangs who'd invariably claim food and resources as their own.

The cities were the worst places to be. Rough sleepers, made homeless by economic collapse, had died in the streets. The smell of rotting bodies, the rats and insanitary conditions, made these places hotbeds of disease, even if you were immune to the plague! The Freedom Seekers were grateful to be in the relative safety of the countryside.

"I'm worried about running out of food," said Leeman to Abraham. "A trade in medicine would give us something to bargain with in the outside world, but nothing's ready yet. I need to do a lot more tests."

"We'll get there," said Abraham. "Be patient. We're managing for now, we have grain stores, root vegetables and winter crops. Spring's just around the corner, then our other crops will grow again."

"I look forward to that. Growing herbs indoors is a real drain on our limited electricity supplies."

"We need to keep our new treatment under wraps for now," said Abraham. "If all the diseased survivors in the country turn up on our doorstep, we'll be overwhelmed and there won't be enough to go around. It has to remain top secret until we're in a better place."

"I've got no argument with that. I wouldn't want to give it out until I'd done more tests and got a good supply going anyway."

Over the weeks that followed, small groups of two or three people from the compound walked to the plantation where the Neem bushes were growing. They returned with bags full of leaves, from which curative compounds could be extracted. But these trips were not without risk. While Jessica and Terry were out, a group of thugs confronted them.

"Lepers! You should be dead," they scowled, "We are the *real* survivors. See?" They bared their arms, "No disease at all. We are the superior race. We are immune! We are the future. The faster we kill all you lepers, the faster we can eliminate the disease and start rebuilding our future." They revealed guns from under their dirty, ragged clothing. Jess and Terry ran for cover.

"Leave them alone!" It was a man's voice and as the ladies turned to look, they saw Alex running towards them from adjacent woodland. He had a gun of his own. He shot at the thugs, sending them on their way, while the girls ran to safety. He looked rough, but ready for a fight.

"I'll catch you later," he said to Jessica, and left the girls to conclude their work.

He appeared outside the Freedom Seekers gates that evening, and Jessica spotted him. She went to speak to him.

"I wanted to find you," she explained, "I never meant to abandon you..." her voice trailed off.

"Don't worry – you're better off here. I understand why I'm not welcome, but I wouldn't want you anywhere else. You must stay here and get well. This is your best chance of survival. The world outside is wretched."

"We may have found a cure," Jessica blabbed the secret. She just couldn't keep the news to herself.

"Really? That's amazing!" he was definitely interested, "What's it made from?"

"It's a type of Neem – some kind of new variety. Created by genetic engineering I think."

"GM is killing the planet!" he looked alarmed.

"Well it's here already, and it's been adapted to enhance its medicinal potential. It turns out it has powerful antifungal qualities."

"Hmm. Not sure I like the sound of it."

"Don't write it off. It's a plant-based medicine, and it's showing a lot of potential as a treatment for this disease. It's supposed to be top secret, but how can I keep something like that to myself!" her eyes sparkled with excitement, and a sneaky grin crept onto her face.

"How come I've not heard of it before?"

"I'm not sure if it's completely new, or just new to the UK, but they say Neem was grown in the tropics, before warming of the planet made it possible to grow it here. It's been used as an Ayurvedic medicine for centuries, but the GM plant has more powerful medicinal properties than the traditional remedy, grows faster, and grows better in this country."

He looked at her suspiciously, as he digested the information.

"I'd still prefer they used non-GM Neem."

"We don't have access to non-GM. The modification helps it grow in the UK, and it grows faster, so it's more prolific than the traditional variety, which means there's plenty to use in medicine. We didn't create it. We're just using what's already there."

"Hmm. OK," he said uneasily. "So what's the plan?"

"We're trying to gather enough of the plant to research it properly, with a view to treating everyone here. We hope to find new pockets of young bushes in the countryside. It grows year round, and grows quickly, so we shouldn't run short."

"Hmm." he shrugged.

"How's life in the real world anyway?" she asked.

"Oh, you know... bleak," he replied. "Gangs everywhere. People want to take the clothes off your back and then kill you. Nasty, to be honest. But I guess I have my freedom, which is something."

"That sounds horrible."

"It *is* horrible. I plan on staying here a while, as the city environment is filthy and disease-ridden, and all the supplies I was relying on have been looted now."

"If you like, you can meet me here at this time every night," suggested Jessica. "I'll let you know of any progress and can pass you any spare supplies. You must have some natural resistance, because you're not showing much sign of infection."

"Oh, my leg's a bit gross," he said. "I'm not immune, sadly."

"Pity. I'll smuggle some out for you when I can. And when I'm better I'll come and join you outside. Stay safe," she smiled warmly and kissed him. Her heart ached. She adored this man and couldn't bear to think of him suffering, alone, in such a hostile world. The feeling was mutual.

Chapter 36
Maximum Potency

The challenge for Leeman and Melluish was to maximise the potency of the genetically enhanced Neem extract, explore its toxicity, and limit the risk of the fungus becoming resistant to it.

"It seems to work topically, but we haven't looked at toxicity. Is it really as non-toxic as it appears?" said Leeman in a morning meeting. "We need to find out."

"That's the big question isn't it," said Melluish. "Can it be safely ingested?"

"Or even applied topically across the whole body - that's a lot of absorption through the skin," said Abraham.

"Can those with debilitating exhaustion and digestive difficulties be cured?" added Melluish.

"A lot of questions," said Leeman. He stood up. "If there's an underlying infection, deep within people's bodies, then the beneficial effect of the topical application will not last. We need to tackle any underlying infections too."

"True. So what next?" asked Abraham.

"Well it's important not to rush it," said Leeman. "Greater chance of long-term survival, if we get it right. Feels like a big responsibility doesn't it!"

"Sure does," Melluish nodded. "When a cure is perfected, the world will need a lot of this stuff! Let's get going!"

Leeman and Melluish worked on maximising the extract's potency, and following weeks of analysis and toxicity testing, it appeared that the compound would be well tolerated by the liver and kidneys, but they needed to be sure. In the absence of lab animals, Leeman considered trying an oral solution on himself. Then he had an idea - there were wild rats living at one end of the compound. He'd catch one or two, see how they responded to a small dose, and work it out from there.

He left some bait in a cage and it proved easy to catch the feisty little rodents, who readily gulped more food laced with the medicine. The rat trial was a success, with no obvious downsides, and the rats were set free to take their chances in the outside world. Leeman was confident enough to consume a little himself. Over 24 hours there were no adverse effects. His blood and urine samples remained normal, so he had growing confidence that the treatment was safe. He decided to try a little bit more. The risks would obviously increase with a higher dose. Again, his body was fine, his toxicity tests, normal. He knew they should proceed with caution, but the only real way of testing both efficacy and toxicity in the human body was to trial it on a larger scale.

"Let me try some?" Jessica offered. "You've increased the potency. It must be nearly ready. I can help you work out the optimal dose."

"OK, soon. Not long now."

"I'm going to take the oral solution daily," he said to Abraham. "So I'm the guinea pig. I'll increase the dose gradually, and take regular blood tests. Then we can see if it's appropriate to offer it to other people."

After a week on the new medicine, he started feeling sick and his symptoms, which had been mild and well controlled by the community's health regime, worsened.

"You look rough!" said Melluish.

"I *feel* rough, but it could be a good sign."

"Always the optimist!"

"No *really*. It's common for the symptoms of a fungal infection to get worse before they get better."

"A healing crisis?"

"Exactly. The dying fungi release toxins into the bloodstream, which makes you feel really bad."

"Ahh yes, of course."

As weeks passed, he continued to feel tired, nauseous, and depressed. His blood tests remained normal, but as the symptoms continued to worsen, he was starting to lose confidence and felt he'd have to review this.

Then overnight his symptoms subsided, and over the next few days, things improved. He had more energy and was feeling much more human.

"I think I'm finally winning!" he said.

158

Elated, he called upon his most enthusiastic volunteers to help with the testing going forward. Jessica eagerly agreed to join the trial. Stephen signed up and Terry volunteered too. She was always willing to try anything.

"You'll probably get terrible 'die-off' symptoms," he warned, "You'll feel worse before you see any improvement. But that's the fungal toxins entering your bloodstream as the fungus dies. I'll start you on a low dose so that you don't experience it too badly," he said.

"OK. I'm ready," Terry said, nervous, but excited.

"Me too!" Jess was buzzing.

Terry took the medicine that evening before bed. She slept badly – her stomach was gurgling and she was too excited to sleep soundly. By the morning she felt worse.

"Oh no. I think I'm going to explode!" She looked miserably at her inflated stomach. "It feels horrible. I'm dizzy."

"Oh crikes. It's affected you really quickly," said Leeman. "Perhaps we should reduce the dose."

"Do you think it's working then?"

"Hard to say. Fungal infections often get worse before they get better, but I think you've reacted more strongly than me, because your infection was worse than mine to start with. Let me take bloods and urine samples so we can see what's going on."

He ran some tests, and found that fermentation of dietary sugars was making her tummy expand, and causing light headedness.

"The fungus is causing fermentation of carbohydrates in your gut," he explained, "so you feel bloated and dizzy. Dying fungi also release toxins, which can cause aching and discomfort. The downsides should subside in due course but we could try a lower dose, so you don't react so badly. Or you could take a break and have a rethink. You don't have to continue, but a lower dose would reduce the risk of adverse reactions."

"OK. Perhaps a night off and then start on a lower dose?" suggested Terry.

"That sounds like a plan."

After a night off, Terry resumed treatment on a low dose, but after a few days, she was at her wit's end. Everything had flared up. Her skin was bleeding where she'd scratched some of the irritating sores. "I don't think it's going to work for me," she sighed miserably, "How long did it take for you?"

"It took a couple of weeks for me to get through the bad patch and start seeing improvements."

"OK. I'll stick with it. My infection is worse than yours. I guess it might take longer to respond?"

"Yes, that's possible. I'd like to do some tests to see how it's affecting your organs. It'll help me assess whether there are any toxicity issues, and see how your liver is coping with the Herxheimer reaction."

"The *what* reaction?"

"The 'die off' reaction - the toxins that make you feel bad as the fungus dies."

"OK."

The tests showed no abnormalities, and Terry's decision to continue was a good move, because a few weeks later she saw some improvement.

She shook her head as she woke up, feeling refreshed for the first time in years. *Am I dreaming? I feel so much better.* She jumped out of bed. *What's happened?* She looked at her body. *Oh my goodness! My skin's improving. I'm healing!* She raced to see Leeman, "I think it's working!"

"Let me see... Oh yes. You're right."

"Look at this! It was red and sore yesterday. Now it's less inflamed."

"Wow! That's fantastic." He ran more tests. The results were very positive. After three weeks, all participants had seen small improvements. Jessica and Stephen saw early signs of their infections starting to recede.

Leeman reported back to Abraham. "The Neem solution, combined with our health regime, is showing great results. It's slow working. We're not out of the woods yet, but everyone on the trial is experiencing fewer symptoms and feeling better for it."

"That's brilliant news," Abraham said. "I should take part too."

"Of course! If you'd like to. There's a period of feeling pretty awful before it improves, but we're working on reducing the intensity of that experience."

"Are there any other issues?"

"Well I'm a bit concerned about supplying demand if word gets out and all the survivors come knocking at our door. The plantations are big, but not infinite."

"Another reason to keep it quiet for now, I think. There are other plantations, miles away, but it's a logistical challenge, and we'd have to work out how to scale up production."

"There is also a real danger of our people meeting renegade gangs while they're out collecting the leaves. Outside, survivors have become savages. We take our lives in our hands every time we step through the gates."

"Hmmm. Yes. I've experienced it too. I'll think about how we can protect ourselves better."

Outside, survivors were angry about the state of the world, aggressive, and willing to kill. Those who were somehow resistant to the disease had energy and firepower. Those who were burdened by the disease, yet still survived outside the compound, were too tired to put up any kind of fight. It was enough of a challenge just to feed themselves. Some committed suicide - a quick end seemed better than slow, painful, starvation.

There was little in the way of clean water, so nasty bacterial infections were rife, killing some of those who hadn't been killed by the fungal epidemic. If you survived the fungus, you could still go down with something else - cholera, typhoid. No one was safe.

People who'd heard about the Freedom Seekers commune and believed in its methods, made their way there, but some died en route. Taking in new people added to the community's burden as they struggled to supply food to all. If new arrivals had signs of other infections, Leeman would offer medicines and sustenance through the gates, refusing to let them in until those symptoms were clear.

The commune had become a new Eden. It was starting to represent a new beginning and a better world. While most of those outside perished, those inside the commune would eventually reach out to create a new world of sustainable living, kindness, self-sufficiency and respect for the planet.

Chapter 37
Dilemma

Jessica had conflicting interests.

"Can you get me some of that medicine yet?" asked Alex during one of their evening liaisons.

"Not at the moment. There's not enough. It's under strict control. But it seems to be working, so we're all on a mission to collect the Neem leaves. Then David Leeman can produce more of the extract. You might benefit from eating the leaves or even putting juice from the crushed leaves on your lesions if that's not too painful?" she suggested. "It's growing in parts of the countryside, so if you see a Neem bush in the wild, you can help yourself. Some of the young bushes are quite small, but just as potent."

"I don't know what it looks like!" he said.

"Oh I'll bring some over to show you," she said. "There's plenty of it about. Our biggest problem is the gangs that threaten us with violence when we're out collecting."

"Bastards."

"Yes, they're horrible. We try to sneak out when they're not around, but you can't always tell."

"That's why I have a gun," he said. "If you're armed you can defend yourself. If you're not, you just have to run for it, and hope you can get away."

Jessica nodded. "Crap isn't it."

*   *   *

Abraham authorised convoys of armed guards to accompany groups of Freedom Seekers making their way to the GM farm to pick Neem leaves from the plantation. But armed groups leaving the compound drew attention to the base and small groups of survivors in the vicinity started to question why the Freedom

Seekers appeared to be in much better health than many of those outside.

Rumours started to spread among groups of survivors that a cure was available inside the facility. Clearly something significant was going on and those outside wanted to know the secrets within.

What were these people after and why did they seem to be healthier than anyone else? What was their secret? Some tentatively approached them outside the commune, to ask.

"We're collecting herbal remedies to support our healthy lifestyle," explained Terry to one elderly lady who seemed immune to the disease.

"Herbal remedies? Does that mean you've found a cure? My son is in a bad way."

"Not yet," Terry replied, feeling guilty. "But we're living very healthy lifestyles and are working to find a cure. When we succeed, it will be made available to everyone!"

"That *is* good news," said the old woman. "I'm doing my best to look after him, but I'm old and resources are scarce. There are no doctors out here, you know. No medicine. Little food - and it's bleak."

"We're experiencing the same problems," she assured the old woman. It was pitiful, but the commune was now at capacity and they were struggling to find enough food and supplies for those already inside. They just couldn't cope with more people.

"I have a secret stash of tinned food in the cellar!" the old woman confessed. "It's keeping us going on rations, until a miracle happens!"

"I'm glad," smiled Terry. "You sound like you're doing well, under the circumstances. It's remarkable that you're unaffected."

"I seem to be immune," she said. "Some of us are immune - that's life I suppose. I used to avoid medicines and never used *hot caffeine.* I wonder if that's why. Some people seem to think the outbreak was caused by our over-dependence on drugs and our addiction to *hot caffeine*! My son was thoroughly addicted to the stuff - a heavy user. Now he's suffering. I'm keeping a safe distance from him, just in case, but it's hard! We're taking every day as it comes."

"Interesting," said Terry. The woman waved her goodbye and went on her way.

Word of the Freedom Seekers' activities had spread to what was left of the government – barely able to call themselves that now, but they were still of the belief that they were in charge. Hiding out in their underground bunker at RAF Air Command in Buckinghamshire, they thought the move would protect them from the disease while they explored possible solutions. But the plan had failed. Men and women in government were experiencing symptoms of the disease and facing the same fate as everyone else.

It didn't take a great deal of surveillance activity for them to find out that within the walls of the commune was a potential cure, which could secure the future of mankind. The secret was held by a man who'd received significant government funding to find a solution, so it should really be in the hands of officials.

"We need their medicine right here, right now," said an advisor to the Prime Minister, "We can't have them wasting precious resources on hippies! We have a job to do."

"I'm not sure they're all hippies," said the Prime Minister, "but I'd agree that we need to preserve the life of our own community first, for the benefit of the whole nation. Perhaps I should go to meet with them and ask for their cooperation. They might willingly provide some of their medicine to help us, if they know where we are."

"I doubt the nicey nicey approach will work sir. I say take it by force."

"But we want them to work with us don't we? Particularly the scientist, Dr Leeman, who developed it – he should be here with us. He's part of the solution and a precious resource. I'll take a car down there tomorrow and talk to them. I'm sure they'll see sense."

The following morning, he did just that. A chauffeur and bodyguard accompanied the Prime Minister to the Freedom Seekers' base.

They stood at the gate and called through. They could see people inside who looked much healthier than those people they'd driven past on their journey. And frankly, they looked much healthier than most people in the bunker too. The Freedom Seekers were succeeding.

The warden on gate duty walked over to see who had arrived, and as recognition crossed his face, he said "Prime Minister?" Aghast.

"Yes," replied the visitor, "I want to meet with your leader."

"I'll go fetch him," the warden said and scampered off.

Abraham went to the gate and let the Prime Minister and his bodyguard inside. "Hello! This is an unexpected surprise!" *We thought the government had come to the same unfortunate end as almost everyone else.* "What can I do for you sir?"

"I've heard you're doing an excellent job here and have discovered a cure for the disease."

Keeping it quiet failed then. Abraham braced himself for an awkward conversation.

"I'd like us to work together," the PM continued, "to make your medicine available to all. But first, we need enough for ourselves – for myself as the leader of the country, for my closest aides, and for others in our bunker. It's a matter of great importance and national security."

"I'm afraid it's not that simple sir. Firstly, we're still testing the treatment. We are conducting trials. Secondly, we have limited production capacity. Thirdly, we work within a very controlled environment, with a focus on healthy lifestyles, and I'm not sure that the treatment will work if these lifestyle elements are not part of the overall healing programme. If you want to learn about them, I am happy to brief you, but you'd have to do it our way if you want access to our precious medicines – which incidentally, are only simple plant extracts."

"Talk me through it please. I'm all ears."

Abraham spent the rest of the morning explaining the intense lifestyle regime that every single person in the compound adopted, as part of their journey to health.

This is ridiculous! thought the Prime Minister. *I don't have time for meditation, relaxation, saunas and alternative therapies – there's a worldwide crisis on our hands. People are dying!* He was irritated.

"Thank you," he said. "I'll give it some thought and come back to you, if I may? Can we take some samples to test anyway? We might be able to show that it's effective, regardless of the lifestyle elements?" He wasn't giving up yet.

"Not this time sir. We don't have any to spare, but stay in touch. We're making progress and will have more news soon."

The Prime Minister didn't look impressed. These people had no right to keep their findings to themselves. As his car departed, he felt enraged. As far as he and the wider government were concerned, there was no one more important than the people in their bunker. If a cure existed, experimental or otherwise, they should be the first to receive it.

It was a few days later when gunmen, under cover of darkness, quietly cut the locks on the gate and forced their way into the facility. Most people were asleep, but Leeman heard the noise and went out to see what the fuss was about.

"We are authorised by the government to confiscate your medicines," said the leader, pointing his machine gun directly at Leeman's face. They had considerable firepower and Leeman wasn't about to argue.

"Hand over your medicines and all your notes," he continued. "We are taking over the project from here. You can work with us, or you can work against us, but there are people more important than you, who need the medicine for the good of the rest of the world. Your commune will have to wait."

"The medicine won't work without the lifestyle interventions," Leeman stressed, and then promptly shut up as a gunman drew closer with his weapon. He handed over all the GM Neem extracts from his lab saying, "I have a very limited supply." They took it and didn't answer.

Leeman pleaded for some understanding as they headed for the door. "I do plan to scale this up," he said. "I plan to roll it out across the world, but it's no use on its own."

"You'll need to speak to the PM. We're just carrying out orders... Got everything boys?"

There was a hum of positivity and they made off with the entire supply of genetically-enhanced Neem that the Freedom Seekers had worked so hard to secure. A few sprigs of Neem on the worktop were all that remained of their work.

"Shit!" he said as the gunmen left. "We're not set up to withstand this kind of anarchy. It's hard enough just to survive! Held at gunpoint by the bloody government!" He was furious.

He slept badly and awoke tired and irritable, but not beaten. "Right," he addressed everyone at morning assembly, "We need

166

to improve our security, and go out collecting more Neem - OK? We all know it's a matter of life and death, but now it seems we're up against the so-called 'government' who want it all for themselves. I don't need the paperwork. I know the extraction method and have copies of the formulas. If you guys can get back out there and put your hearts and souls into collecting the leaves, we can manufacture more of the medicine and continue our trials. You know what to do."

After a few days of further thought, Leeman cooled down and considered the bigger picture. "I am a little bit tempted to work with the government," he said to Melluish, "just so that we can pool resources, increase production and maximise the benefit of our work."

"Yeah, but their approach of turning up in the dead of night with guns, and stealing our medicine doesn't help their case, does it."

"It's totally out of order and it infuriated me. But I can see, on a more civilized level, that it could make sense to work together."

"That might depend on what they have to offer."

"They could make life very difficult for us, if we don't."

"That's true - if they carry on throwing their weight around like that."

"I just feel really irritated that these stupid, narrow-minded people are too bloody-minded to see that the treatment probably won't work without the lifestyle interventions. They're stealing from those who've put in the work and have a chance, to give the medicine to those, who frankly, are going to die anyway. Bastards."

The government officials were so set in their old predictable ways, wanting a quick solution - a magic bullet. That was what had led to the fungal epidemic in the first place – a toxic culture of unhealthy living, a reliance on pharmaceutical drugs rather than healthy living, destroying the planet, and allowing the pathogenic fungus to thrive. *Total bloody morons.*

Chapter 38
Resuming Work

With new stocks of GM Neem collected by dedicated members of the Freedom Seekers, Leeman started to manufacture the remedy again. He wasn't going to be beaten by the bulldozer tactics of jumped-up government officials who didn't understand how the treatment worked. He gave the first batch produced to those most in need, and Terry was one very grateful recipient. As the trial resumed, monitoring continued.

Leeman met with Abraham to discuss the possibility of pooling resources with the government. "Melluish has agreed to take over the laboratory work in the commune if I want to meet with the PM or work from another base," he explained.

"OK. Well I'm happy for you to explore the options."

"I'll go and talk to them. If we pool resources we might make faster progress, which would be beneficial for everyone."

He turned up outside Air Command in Buckinghamshire. All was quiet. He approached the guard on the gate, who pointed a gun at him.

"I'm David Leeman," he said tentatively. "The PM came to speak to me about a cure for the epidemic. I'm ready to talk about a partnership. Can I see someone?"

The guard grunted, "I need to radio and find out." He disappeared into his guard box, still holding his gun ready, as if he anticipated the scientist might turn rogue. Two minutes later he stepped back outside, "Someone will come to collect you."

Leeman waited patiently. Then an Officer walked through the tall security gates, "Dr Leeman?"

"Yes."

"I'm here to take you to see the Prime Minister."

They walked through RAF Air Command, a big site. It took about five minutes to reach the bunker. Leeman followed the Officer through the dirty green entrance, partially obscured by foliage.

They went deep underground, through blast doors, and entered long whitewashed tunnels. Their footsteps echoed as they walked.

Upon reaching the meeting room, the Prime Minister was waiting. "I hoped you'd change your mind and come to work with us Dr Leeman," he said.

"I'm open to discussions," he replied. "But if the gunmen that broke into our facility really were sent by the government, I'm disgusted by your approach. I'm not sure I want to work with people like that!"

"I apologise for our heavy-handedness, but we felt it was necessary," said the PM. "We don't have the time to participate in many of the therapies you advise. We're in the middle of a global crisis and can't be seen to be wasting time on yoga, meditation and such follies. We wanted the drug to help save some of our brightest minds and important contributors - some of the people who can sort out this mess and rebuild society. However, so far, there's no evidence that your cure works."

"No it doesn't work. I told you that! And I told your tough guys that!"

"My recollection was that you weren't sure."

"OK - that's true. We have *strong suspicions* that if you don't make the lifestyle changes to harness the full potential of your immune systems, then the cure won't work. Look, you haven't been using it for long and you don't have a lot of supplies, but my feeling is that it's not the magic bullet you're after. However, if we work together, perhaps we can achieve the results you want by pooling our skills and resources. What do you say?"

"That sounds like a way forward," said the PM. "How would you envisage that working?"

Leeman looked thoughtful. "I'm not willing to abandon the commune, but if we can work in a way that benefits us both and is more productive for everyone in the long run, then I'm prepared to discuss it."

"OK. Let me show you our facilities." He led Leeman down the hallway to a state-of-the-art laboratory with every conceivable piece of equipment inside. "This would be your laboratory. As you can see, the equipment alone, is far superior to anything you've been using and will hasten your progress. We can also provide support."

"And in exchange?"

"We want the medicine obviously - a potent version that will help everyone, regardless of lifestyle. I'm sure when you're up and running, and the recipe is perfected, there'll be enough to go around. The ultimate aim is to blast this disease out of existence with a powerful drug that kills it dead in its tracks."

"That's a big ask."

"It is, and we believe you're the person to deliver it, Dr Leeman. Are you up to the challenge?"

"I believe I am," he replied, "but it's conditional upon me continuing my work with the Freedom Seekers."

"We can live with that," said the PM.

"OK. I'll need to give more thought as to how we proceed."

"Don't take too long Dr Leeman – we all know the situation is critical."

He nodded and the Officer who brought him in, stepped up to escort him back across the base. They chatted as they walked through the grounds. "They're not being difficult you know. The government really doesn't have time for big lifestyle changes."

"Yes, I can see that."

"And most people are just trying to survive."

"Yes, I get it. People on the streets are struggling to feed themselves."

"So, while we all admire your holistic approach, it's just not practical for most people in the modern world."

"Yes," he admitted. "I do understand. I will do my very best." He felt overwhelmed by the challenges and responsibilities that lay ahead.

"We have a lot of faith in you, Dr Leeman," the Officer waved him off. As the scientist drove back to his commune, he hoped their faith wasn't misplaced.

He tossed and turned that night. He knew the government was right. People didn't have the will, the capacity, or the resources to change their lifestyles – particularly in the current circumstances. They needed a quick fix, just to get everything back to normality – or as close to normality as possible. If he wanted to save people outside his own commune, then he needed to develop a stronger drug with more practical applications, and it needed to work quickly. Was that even possible? He didn't know, but he felt compelled to try.

Chapter 39
Working in Partnership

Back at the commune Leeman called a meeting, inviting all the Freedom Seekers to attend. He explained the situation. "The government is operating from an underground bunker at RAF Air Command, and the Prime Minister has offered me excellent resources to develop our research. This would benefit everyone – both inside the commune and outside in the wider world. The downside is it means I'd need to spend time over in the military bunker, where the laboratory is based."

"You can't leave us!" someone cried out.

"I would not be abandoning the commune, it just means I won't be here as much. Jonathan Melluish will stay here, producing the medicinal extract we've been working on and upscaling production, so there's more to go around."

"How can they be the government anyway?" another person piped up. "The government went bankrupt ages ago and no one's been elected in years!"

"An emergency government was formed during the pandemic, and they still seem to control a small military and have some government resources. The partnership simply means we can pool resources for our mutual benefit."

There was a hum as people absorbed the news. Some were pleased with the development, others less convinced.

"The trials so far have been a huge success," he continued, "so it's time to bring you all in on the action and roll out the treatment to anyone who wants it. Total cure takes time, but you should start to see the benefits in weeks. There are some unpleasant side-effects early on. When the fungus starts to die, symptoms might get worse and this can make you feel terrible. So starting the treatment on a low dose with some caution and managing your expectations is advisable. However, the early results have been very good - let's see if we can get this whole community well again."

There was a clap and a cheer from the members, with many nods of agreement.

Leeman continued, "I feel that trying to help more people, if that's possible, is the right thing to do. We should try to help, even if we fail. I hope you can all understand and support me on this. Melluish will organise ongoing collections of the Neem, and our attempts to grow Neem within our community is starting to show results."

There was a hum of conversation among the crowd. No one protested, although some were sorry to see him leave.

*   *   *

Leeman worked with the government over six long months to engineer a medicine that was much stronger, more potent, and faster working. The resulting drug was a combination of the GM Neem extract, combined with the most potent antifungals ever developed, including those tried and abandoned due to safety concerns. Anti-parasitic chemicals were added, to increase its effectiveness. The combination made the final drug very toxic, and the technicians needed to establish whether the human liver could break down the different elements and eliminate them safely. It would certainly be too risky for anyone with compromised liver function.

They pondered the best way to test the new drug. There were diseased animals roaming the streets – stray cats, dogs and hundreds of rodents. The animals were worn down, emaciated, desperate. It meant that finding test subjects was easy. The technicians lured a few stray pets into boxes with food. Their owners had passed away, so no one missed them. Then, back at the lab, they gave the animals some of the new drug in some pet food. They gulped it down and drifted off into a contented sleep.

The following morning they were all dead. Every single one. Liver failure as best the technicians could tell. This was going to be a long process.

They went back to the drawing board. How could they make it less toxic but still powerful? Months of further research ensued, tweaking the medicinal compounds, removing those deemed too toxic, and working with new components that they hoped would add potency. It was after one of the PM's most trusted aides died from the disease that he came down to the lab himself.

"Haven't you made any progress yet? You've been working on this for months! We've persevered using your plant extract, to little effect. I've just lost one of my colleagues to the disease. Whatever new drug you have available, we need it now."

Leeman looked anxious. He didn't want to harm anyone, and these substances were still risky, but they had taken out the most toxic elements. Perhaps it was time for testing again.

* * *

In the commune, the Freedom Seekers had seen considerable improvement by using the Neem extract, in combination with their health regime. Leeman scaled up production of the extract in the government lab, while Melluish continued to oversee its use within the commune.

Government personnel assisted with Neem collections. It was just as well the plants were fast growing, evergreen, and new bushes seeded themselves in the countryside over the spring and summer. It was plentiful.

"I feel so much better," said Abraham. "It's great to have got rid of some of the horrible flaky skin and sores."

"It's going so well," replied Leeman, "but some people are frightened of the disease getting worse again, developing resistance. We should be OK as long as we stick to the regime, but these things can take a long time to clear completely."

"How long?"

"It could take years."

"Really?"

"I hope not, but it's possible."

"Oh well. I'm in it for the long haul anyway. Not sure I'll ever want to eat a sticky bun ever again!"

They stuck to the natural remedy and the health regime. It was no hardship. Many inside had never felt so positive and contented with their lifestyle.

Stephen and Jessica were seeing their infections slowly fade and they were feeling a lot better than they did when they arrived. Terry was still struggling with the systemic nature of her infection, which was proving more difficult to shift. However, as she persevered with the regime, she saw measurable improvement.

173

Sometimes, these things just take time. Mark and Kevin? They were "chillin'" and happy to see their skin improving as they stuck to the health programme.

* * *

Inside the bunker, Leeman met with the PM: "So you're impatient for the latest drug? I understand, but it's just as well we didn't rush the process because the first version would have killed people."

"That was months ago. Where are we now?"

"We're in a better position now. I'm ready to test a new drug combination, with lower toxicity. We'll test it on street animals and if all goes well, it'll be available for human trials soon.

The PM nodded. "I'm glad to hear it. If you need anything, just ask. Thank you Dr Leeman."

Remarkably, a few days after administration with the new drug, the diseased street animals started to perk up. Visible signs of their fungal infections reduced. More testing ensued and the results were consistent.

"We've had a breakthrough!" said Leeman to the PM. "We've treated 50 animals over the past three weeks, and they're all as good as new. We released the animals with a new lease of life, and they all left looking better than when they came in.

"We don't know the long-term effects, but in the short-term, it appears to be a very effective treatment," he continued. "And on that basis, as it's an emergency situation, I'm prepared to try this on people, if you still want to?" He looked at the PM. "It's risky. This is fast-tracked and it goes against normal protocols, but if you want to find out if it works on people, sooner rather than later, then we're in a good position to proceed with caution."

The PM nodded in agreement. "OK. Let's do this. We have a man who is virtually on his death bed. I expect he'll volunteer."

He did. Along with a military man who'd succumbed to the disease and was in a bad way. "OK. Let's begin with a very small dose," said Leeman, as the two gentlemen joined him in the government's underground lab.

* * *

When he returned to the Freedom Seekers that night, Terry was itching to hear about their progress. "Let me take part!" she pleaded when she heard the news.

"If you're sure," he said. "There's still a risk."

"I'm sure."

Later that week half a dozen people, Terry included, took a small dose of the new medicine. They took blood tests to assess their progress. The results were remarkable. There was little sign of toxicity, and the medicine demonstrated effectiveness after just a couple of days. The skin problems started to visibly clear and those taking part started to feel better. There was no need to stick to any health regime - it was working among those in the government bunker too. The only limitation was the availability of some of the pharmaceutical ingredients. That could become a big problem down the line, but time would tell. The trial was a huge success.

Now they needed more of the drug to keep up the good work. The development process was a lot more complicated than the Neem plant extract. Where could they get some of those limited pharmaceutical supplies?

"The obvious place to start is the old drug companies," suggested Abraham. "Pharmaceutical supplies might be locked up in the derelict buildings and warehouses, once used by the drug companies. It's got to be worth investigating."

"That's a good idea," said Leeman. "I can make some of what we need from scratch but I still need raw materials, and having some of the ingredients to hand would certainly speed up progress."

Coordinated raids of derelict pharmaceutical companies began. Raw ingredients were obtained by whatever means necessary - cultivation, negotiation or force. There were no big companies trading - just a few independent chemists serving small local communities as best they could, and they left those traders alone.

The government officials made contact with surviving farmers, with a view to getting them to save seed and grow the crops needed for the raw materials used in the medicine - not just Neem, but other plants used to create pharmaceutical compounds too. They promised to help farmers with agricultural supplies, security, and manpower.

"How come you're able do this?" asked Leeman one day. "Considering you're bankrupt."

"We have resources," explained the PM. "People committed to helping us, a dedicated military who are still being housed, fed and provided for, access to modest funds. Don't you worry about that. We have ways of getting things done."

In return for their cooperation, the farmers were promised all the support they needed, and supplies of the cure when it was ready. Within weeks, the infrastructure was in place to secure an ongoing supply of the active ingredients, and Leeman had enough essential ingredients in-house to begin production on a bigger scale, alongside a dedicated team.

However, when the first supplies of the new medicine became available, it was clear that decisions had already been made. The drug would be used to support an elite population inside the bunker only. They wouldn't let Leeman take any supplies to his commune.

"You're telling me that everyone outside this bunker is expendable?" he asked furiously.

"That's not what we said," said the PM.

"You're just refusing to help anyone else."

"Only for the time being - until our own people are fully recovered."

"That's totally outrageous. You help my people or I quit!" he said.

"As you wish," said the PM.

Chapter 40
Light at the End of the Tunnel

It was crystal clear that at least in the short term, the government planned to keep the cure for themselves. They weren't going to help the wider community any time soon. They'd got what they wanted from Leeman, who left the bunker to resume his position with the Freedom Seekers. The government excluded him from further discussions, confiscated his notes and formulae. They weren't prepared to discuss it. He felt exploited and aggrieved.

"I've got a pretty good idea how to recreate the medicine," he said to Melluish, "but I don't have the equipment or the resources to develop it here."

"Perhaps the government will come round. I expect they'll want your help again at some point."

"It really pisses me off. What a despicable lot. Not sure I *want* to work with them again."

"You may have no choice. How are you faring after the trials anyway?"

"I treated myself with the new drug and my symptoms have gone completely. There's no doubt it's miraculous. That's what makes it all the more infuriating - they're being so selfish. It's so wrong."

"Try not to feel bad about it. I guess it's similar to our reluctance to offer medicines to the wider world until we've got everything under control in the commune."

"Yes, but I've been working with them to develop it. They couldn't have done it without me."

"True. Look, on the bright side, we've been very successfully finding new pockets of GM Neem growing in the countryside, and our supply here is growing well."

"True. I'll try to think positive and we'll do what we can from here."

They continued with their natural, holistic regime and Leeman and Melluish continued to make as much of the healing plant extract as they could muster. Terry was in much better shape, having fought off the worst of the disease with a combination of Neem and a spell on the powerful drug trial. She hoped all symptoms would fade completely in time, but either way, she couldn't complain. She felt so much better.

The Neem extract offered a healing lifeline to all members of the commune. They'd all been taking it while Leeman was away and they'd all improved. People were slowly getting better. It was slow compared to the speed and ferocity of the new drug that Leeman had created in the government lab, but it was undoubtedly safer.

The Freedom Seekers had now developed such a reputation for wellness that it had become almost biblical. The commune was seen as 'the promised land'. People believed it was the only place on earth where you could be assured of a cure from the epidemic, and a future life of health and happiness.

"We've got refugees who've travelled hundreds of miles to reach us, but no room!" said Abraham. "I don't know what to do. We don't have the space or resources to help everyone. They've started setting up encampments outside, hoping to be offered a cure and a place inside."

"I think they'll need to set up a commune of their own," said Leeman. "We can help and advise them, but we're full to the brim here, we just can't take more people. We've already got people crashing on mattresses on the floor of the assembly hall, and it's starting to compromise the regime, which is no help to anyone."

Abraham went to speak to the people camping outside the gates. "If you want to live like us, you need to set up a community of your own," he explained. "We can advise you, but we are not in a position to invite you all inside. We don't have the resources, and our buildings and facilities are already full to capacity. We struggle to find enough food to feed ourselves, much less provide for other people, but we'll help you where we can."

"Please let us in!" a woman begged.

"I'm sorry, but no," Abraham continued. "We will help you with advice, and supply any resources we can spare. But that's all we can offer at the moment. We'll help you get started and support you."

She cried, while other refugees muttered discontentedly.

"Look come on!" said a scruffy man among the group. "He said they'll help us. We can set up our own commune and work with these people. Let's be optimistic about this. It's the way of the Freedom Seekers. No doom and gloom. We must think positive!"

The weeping woman looked up at him, confusion in her eyes. "Really? You think we can do this?"

"Of course we can."

"Many of us are really unwell." She was right of course. Many looked too tired and ill to care.

"We'll do what we can," continued Mr Positive. "Let's build our own community and our own regime, to bring better health and boost our natural immunity."

He turned to Abraham, "Is there anything we can do to assist you?"

"There's no need. You have enough problems of your own," he replied.

"We'd like to help!"

"Well, you can collect Neem leaves if you like," said Abraham. "It'll help speed things up so we can supply you with the extract, more quickly. And we'll help you adopt some basic lifestyle measures, as these things work together for the most benefit."

Small groups of Freedom Seekers went out to see people in the refugee camp, to teach them some of the methods that had helped to boost people's immunity in the commune.

Inspired refugees with reasonable health, set up a base at an abandoned farmhouse nearby, but there wasn't room for everyone, so many remained camped outside the Freedom Seekers commune, trying to embrace a healthy new lifestyle in less than ideal conditions. They foraged for food in woodland and explored agricultural land for edible crops. Some of the plants they returned with were tough but edible. It was a start.

They set up a self-sufficient farming community of their own and tried to replicate the Freedom Seekers' way of life. But they were plagued by gangs, struggling to feed themselves, and life was hard. It was not the healthy, restful environment that they were trying to achieve. The refugees felt empowered to help themselves, but it wasn't enough.

Leeman travelled back out to see the Prime Minister. There were so many people in need. Ignoring them was not an option.

179

The PM didn't want to see him, but one of his aides reluctantly agreed to talk.

"We've got refugees camping outside our gates!" Leeman was exasperated, "We can't help everyone. We need government support. They just want food and a cure. They're desperate."

"We will provide medicine for other people in good time, but for now, with limited amounts available, we need to prioritise."

"Prioritise my arse!" said Leeman.

"We must ensure the survival of the very brightest and best of mankind."

"That's ridiculous!" Leeman scolded angrily. "You cannot decide who lives and who dies."

"Oh, but we can," said the official. "It's at times like this, that it's the responsibility of the government to make these hard decisions - to direct resources where they'll offer the greatest long-term benefits to society."

"There will be no 'society' left unless we move quickly!" said Leeman in an icy tone. "This is not the end of the matter."

Back at the gates of the Freedom Seekers, he stood up and spoke to the growing numbers of refugees outside. "The government has a powerful cure for the disease, which doesn't rely on lifestyle changes, but they're refusing to share it, due to limited availability. I've asked them to help you, but they're stubborn, and keeping a low profile in their bunker at Air Command. I'm hoping the situation will change soon."

"Selfish bastards!" a woman shouted angrily.

"Will they even speak with us?" said another, exasperated.

"I'm having trouble getting them to speak to me," said Leeman, "but there's nothing to stop you protesting outside their gates."

A man spoke up. "That'd be pointless. I've seen the place. The guards there have guns. You won't get anywhere."

"It's true," said Leeman. "I cannot think of another way of putting pressure on them. There are no communications."

"We don't have the energy for a fight with government officials who are determined not to help," he said. "We'll stay put, continue to work with you guys, and hopefully we'll see better health eventually." There was a murmur of agreement.

A few weeks later, as dusk fell, a woman arrived at the gates of the Freedom Seekers. "Hello? I want to help you," she called through. Leeman approached her. She was in good shape – not diseased like other people outside. "I've heard about your work with the government, and their refusal to share it. I have access to excellent laboratory facilities and can provide the proper equipment and source any pharmaceutical supplies needed to help you recreate that powerful new cure in abundance."

"Really?" Leeman was surprised, excited, and a bit sceptical. "This is very unexpected. Can we back track a bit? Who are you?" He invited her inside.

"I'm Kate, and I'm an ex-army Colonel. I fell out badly with the government after they wanted to selectively save all the bigwigs and VIPs while leaving everyone in the rest of the country to die. They offered me and some of my colleagues a place in their bunker but we refused and formed our own survivors' group above ground." She looked irritated, even as she spoke about it, then continued, "I hear many of the government's top people have already passed away from the disease — so their methods didn't save them, although they may have delayed its progress. Perhaps that's how they made it this far. I'm lucky — I haven't contracted the disease. I have no idea why, but I intend to make the most of my good health to help other people."

"I'm so pleased you've made contact," said Leeman.

"Thank you. Our small community - some military colleagues and a few friends - is located on the Welsh border. I wanted to make contact and offer our facilities for mutual benefit. We have a state-of-the-art laboratory, but no one skilled or talented enough to use it properly. I think with our equipment and your genius we could make a real difference."

"Wow!" he said. "I'm blown away! That sounds perfect! I'll come and have a look!"

"Please do. We'd be delighted to have you. Stay for a while, so we can start work on a cure."

"I'll need to discuss what happens here if I travel to Wales, but let me speak to my colleagues."

She nodded, "Yes of course. I didn't expect you to leave with me right away, but if you do have a place where I can crash for the night, then that would be wonderful, and I'll head back in the morning… or I can wait a while longer, if you'd like to come with me?"

He took a moment to think, "You can sleep on the sofa," he offered apologetically. "We don't have spare beds." She smiled, grateful for anywhere that was comfortable.

The following morning, Leeman awoke feeling invigorated. He checked with Abraham and Melluish, "Is me leaving again all right?"

"You go!" said Melluish. "We can continue without you. We're pretty self-sufficient these days!"

"We'll need to take supplies of the Neem up there...." said Leeman.

"You could, to get started, but there's another plantation on the outskirts of the Forest of Dean, so you could get supplies there in the longer term," said Melluish.

"Really? That's brilliant!"

"There are a few about," he said. "The plantations were created around the UK to see where the GM Neem grew most prolifically. The researchers anticipated needing a good supply of the plant for use in medicine, so you'll find it in strategic locations across the country, which might be useful in the future."

"That's excellent. It'll certainly make production of the medicine much easier."

Melluish smiled. "Happy to help."

"OK. Let's do it," he said to Kate. "I need a few hours to sort things out here, but we can leave after lunch, if that suits you." He packed a bag and left with Kate that afternoon. "Do you have supplies of petrol or diesel?" he asked.

"The jeep runs on vegetable oil and there's plenty of that around. Even hungry people feel sick if they drink too much oil, so there are warehouses full of the stuff that no one wants... unless they have an oil-powered vehicle of course. There are a few of us around!"

Just over two hours passed and they reached a small isolated community, being run along military quarantine lines. "This is it," she said, as the man on the gate let them pass. They walked through a commune with tall gates and military style security. There were small wind turbines, solar panels, and an emergency generator on the site. It was similar to the Freedom Seekers' arrangement, but smaller and without the rigorous health regime.

They walked across the yard, to a very ordinary looking red brick building. Kate opened the door and beckoned him in. "This is our state-of-the-art laboratory," she said proudly. Inside was a sparkling clean facility full of the latest equipment and technology.

"This is excellent!" said Leeman, as he surveyed the room and picked up some of the equipment for closer inspection. "We'll need a plan of action to get the materials we need... not least, the pharmaceutical supplies, GM Neem, and a team to support me in the lab. I'm told there's a GM Neem plantation in the Forest of Dean, so we'd better go and find it."

Kate clapped her hands, "Perfect!"

"The pharmaceutical supplies will be trickier to get," he cautioned. "The government had farmers on hand to grow some raw materials and they raided old drugs companies for pharmaceutical supplies."

"That's not a problem. We can do the same," said Kate. "We have some pharmaceutical supplies already, so we have a head start."

"We'll need a work party to collect the Neem," he added.

"We can get that started as soon as we're fully briefed."

"OK. Great!" said Leeman.

"Now let me show you your quarters." She beckoned him to follow.

"I have quarters?" He said with a smile, and followed her to a modern minimalist flat. It was refreshingly smart and something of a contrast to the old boarding school dormitories that the Freedom Seekers used. He slept well, in awe of the possibilities.

As morning dawned, he was awakened by an alarm call that woke the entire community. They rose in military style, turning up half an hour later for breakfast, and then work.

Kate explained, "We work very efficiently here. These men (she pointed to a small group, drinking their morning coffee at a table) will help you source the ingredients you need. I've selected our brightest scientific minds to help you in the lab. We have access to pharmaceutical supplies in an abandoned warehouse in Cardiff. There's a supply of basic drugs here on site too, but whatever you need, just shout, and we'll head out to pick up supplies."

"OK. Great!" said Leeman.

He briefed the team and by lunchtime, the lads had been down to the Forest of Dean collecting Neem and returned with an abundance of the leaves to start work. They also planted some Neem saplings within the Welsh commune.

"You don't mess about do you?" said Leeman, amazed by what they brought back. "This is great!"

"The saplings should grow quickly with all our Welsh rain!" said Kate.

"They grow quickly anywhere," he grinned.

Chapter 41
Making Progress

Over the course of the next couple of months, Leeman and his new team tried to recreate the formula from his memories of the process in the government lab. Every time the scientist thought he'd cracked the formula, he tested it on stray animals, lured into the facility looking for food, but the medicine had little effect. He'd got the toxicity levels right - they seemed unharmed, blood and urine tests were normal - but they weren't cured either. He was frustrated.

"I need to return to the Freedom Seekers," he said, "because then I can speak to the government scientists to try to find out where I'm going wrong."

He set off and the Freedom Seekers were delighted to welcome him back.

"Welcome home!" said Terry, throwing her arms around him. "We were a little concerned. It's been so long!" She was looking much better, he thought. The progress with this extract was slow but sure. "Nice to see you too. You're looking good!" he said.

She grinned. "Thank you." Blushed.

"How is everyone?" he asked.

"They're good. We're keeping up the regime. Still feeling better. Most people are on the mend. How's the place in Wales?"

"You wouldn't believe the facilities!" he enthused. "They're excellent, but I can't figure out what I'm doing wrong. I don't have the formula from the government experiments. They wouldn't let me take anything out of there, but something is missing."

"Are you going to ask the government for help then?"

"Yes. It makes sense to try. There's a good supply of GM Neem in Wales. There's no reason not to share knowledge."

He set off to see the government the following morning, but the PM was dismissive and refused to see him.

"Look," he pleaded, snatching the guard's radio at the entrance. "We can help each other. There's another plantation of GM Neem in the Forest of Dean, and it's growing really well there. We have pharmaceutical supplies and Welsh farmers helping us with raw ingredients. This will help resolve some of your supply problems. PLEASE, just hear me out."

The news piqued the PM's interest as the risk of supplies running short was a pertinent issue. Suddenly the PM's voice came through: "You say there's a plentiful supply in Wales? OK... come through and we'll talk."

"At last!" Leeman sighed. He waited for an escort and then went through the heavily armed gates, accompanied by an Officer, to the bunker.

This face to face meeting with the PM had to count, as it might be his last. He tried to explain the problem. "There are hundreds of refugees settled near our commune who may die if they don't get treatment," he explained. "I have a new lab and I'm trying to recreate the cure, but I can't remember the formula. Something isn't right. Can I have access to the scientific notes and the formula I made while working for you? Surely you don't want your citizens to needlessly die? This won't affect your own supply. It will have no impact at all on your own project."

The PM looked deep in thought, "I'll send a man over to verify your statement this afternoon. He'll pick you up from the Freedom Seekers at one o'clock and you can drive up to Wales together."

"Aren't you going to let me have the formula?" asked Leeman.

"Not until your story has been verified."

Leeman felt irritated but restrained himself and went along with the charade.

Back at the Freedom Seekers compound, Leeman was starting to feel excited. If the government *would* cooperate, the formula could enable him to eradicate the disease around the world! One region at a time, anyway.

"If all goes well," he said to Terry, "I see no reason why we shouldn't have a proper cure for everyone who needs it, eventually. This is going to be hard work, but it's very exciting!"

"That's amazing! I just hope we don't lose you to the Welsh!" she said.

"You're not going to lose me. Besides, you won't need me once this crisis is over!

"Oh I'm sure we can use your skills. I like having you around," she grinned.

"I like you too," he said. A sparkle in his eye.

She smiled awkwardly, looked away as she felt her cheeks burn, then looked back at him, shyly.

He smiled. "When the disease is eradicated, we can start to rebuild our society again."

She nodded. "Good to maintain the healthy lifestyles though. Feels good."

"Oh definitely," he agreed. "Keeping our immune systems in good shape will be important over the next few years. With all the death and disease out there, the risk of infection from something is never far away. As we try to rebuild society, it's going to be a really challenging time."

"Do you think the government will give you the formula?"

"I suspect they'll come round. Think positive." They smiled at one another warmly.

*   *   *

As promised, Sgt Regan from the government bunker, turned up at 1pm. He acknowledged the refugee camp outside, and they set off to the lush green hills of Wales.

As they approached the Welsh border, Leeman pointed out the Neem plantation and fields of medicinal crops grown by local farmers. Kate met them at the entrance to the compound and introduced herself.

"This is excellent!" said Sgt Regan.

"We have a network of suppliers across Wales and the borders," explained Kate. "We have resources well beyond what you can see here. There's plenty for everyone. We can help each other."

Sgt Regan smiled. Their progress looked very promising. "Come and see the lab," she continued. The men followed her to the lab, and Sgt Regan looked in awe at the equipment, which was every bit as good as what they were using in the bunker.

"You're very well equipped!" he said, surprised by their achievements. "I've been told, if it all checks out, to give you the formula," he added. He pulled some papers out of his jacket pocket. "This is the formula for the medicine you helped us develop - some of your notes are there too. I hope it's everything you need."

Leeman inspected the papers and a big smile crept onto his face. "Thank you!" he said, still taking in the fullness of what this meant.

"I'm sorry we've been so evasive but we had to make tough decisions," said Sgt Regan, "and we didn't take them lightly. We were afraid of spreading resources so thinly that no one really benefited in the long term. But you're no threat to our survival. As you say, we can help each other."

Leeman was relieved, "Don't worry. I get it. I was faced with the same dilemma when refugees started setting up camp outside our facility, looking for food and medicine – we could barely feed ourselves and were struggling to make enough of our herbal medicine to meet demand within the commune. But the new arrivals helped us to gather Neem, and with their support we upscaled production, so we were able to help each other in the end. We're doing what we can to ease their suffering, but I do wish we could do more." He looked at the papers again, solemnly, and continued, "It's tough. I too, had to make that difficult decision to help my own people first, for the greater good. There simply weren't enough resources to save everyone. I'm hopeful that's about to change."

Leeman stayed in Wales and waved goodbye to Sgt Regan, promising to stay in touch. He left in a military vehicle that had been sent to collect him. It was a very supportive and civilized exchange, considering the previous animosity between the two parties.

"There's nothing to stop us now," he said to Kate, "unless we have a supply problem, but I'm hoping we can overcome such challenges."

"Agreed," she said. "High Five!" and they slapped hands together, enjoying the moment of victory.

There was a loud and jovial cheer when others at the Welsh commune heard the good news. The lab team soon got together for a briefing. As they prepared the first batch in strict accordance with the formula, there was an air of excitement and anticipation. The future looked so much brighter. People could envisage making plans, which might have seemed fanciful before.

However the rebuilding of civilisation would be a massive task. With society in ruins, and the country characterised by ghost towns and renegade gangs, a return to anything resembling normality would be a long and overwhelming journey.

Chapter 42
New Trials

Within a couple of weeks the first supplies were ready.

"You promised us the first batch," said Kate keenly.

"I certainly did and I'm not going to let you down. Bring me your worst affected people and let's get them onto the medication. You'll be delighted. I know you will."

Kate brought half a dozen of her most diseased community members to meet Leeman, and one at a time, he assessed their conditions. They were in a bad way, exhausted, so drained by the infection that they could barely function.

"There may be side effects to this medication, and your condition may worsen for a short while before it gets better," he warned, prior to giving a poorly man his first dose. The patient looked worried.

"Worsen?" he mumbled, fear in his eyes.

"Don't worry, it's fast acting, so you shouldn't be down for too long. I'll start with a low dose, so it's not putting too much pressure on your liver."

"OK," he said. Still worried.

"It might make you want to sleep for a few days, but just take it easy. Get all the rest you need. Then you'll start to see a gradual improvement. You may still have times when you feel rough, but these will become fewer over time. Your skin will clear. You'll start to feel more like your old self. Are you ready to give it a go?"

He nodded forlornly.

"You don't look convinced. Would you rather go onto a natural health regime to manage the symptoms and boost your immune system? You can have a rethink about using the medication later if you feel more up to it? There's no pressure here."

"No," he said quietly. I want to feel better as fast as possible. I'm more concerned about safety."

"Oh I see. Well, it's being used by the government, and they've had excellent results from it. I've used it myself, and that's why I no longer have any signs of disease." He rolled his sleeves up and showed off his arms, with a grin. "I have every confidence in it or I wouldn't be suggesting we use it here. But the decision is yours. It's entirely up to you whether you want to accept treatment."

"I'd like to go ahead. Thanks," he nodded.

Leeman watched the diseased man take his first dose and return to his room to rest. Then he saw the others, one by one, for a chat about the side effects, and whether they wanted to go ahead with treatment. The next few days were fraught with tension as everyone waited to see what would happen.

As predicted, some of those treated slipped into decline, seeing their symptoms worsen, but this was short-lived. After a couple of days, they started to perk up. Within a week, they were all showing signs of having more energy, with fewer symptoms, and the ugly sores, growths and lesions on the skin were starting to heal.

"I'm so impressed!" said Kate. "It's only been a couple of weeks, and the people who've had treatment are all up and about, feeling and looking better."

"Great isn't it!" said Leeman. "I predict that if they continue with the treatment, after a couple of months they'll almost be back to normal, looking healthier, feeling like they've been given a new lease of life."

"Fingers crossed," she said, buzzing.

"We do need to monitor participants closely," said Leeman, "but I think we can now treat others on the basis of this result. Agreed?"

"Absolutely." They ramped up production to maximum capacity.

A couple of weeks later, he returned to the Freedom Seekers with a supply of the medicine, and was immediately faced with an unexpected dilemma. Refugees camped outside the commune looked wretched. They were staying positive and trying to help themselves, but it wasn't very effective, primarily because they were living in a hostile environment, without the controls and safety of the commune. They needed the drugs more than the Freedom Seekers. He didn't have enough for everyone.

Walking through the encampment of desperate people outside, Leeman went inside the commune to discuss the dilemma with

Abraham. "I don't know what to do!" he said. "The Freedom Seekers have their symptoms under control, sort of. The people outside do not. They are more ill and more desperate than we are. But I feel an obligation to the people inside, who've been working with us for years, shown immense commitment to the health regime, and had never expected anything in return, except to feel better for it. Some are still struggling with symptoms, and this drug could give them the final boost they need. What do you think I should do?"

"How long will it take to create more of this stuff?" asked Abraham.

"It shouldn't take long. It took us a couple of weeks to produce this first batch - which was split with the Welsh commune."

"There's no shortage of the chemicals you need to produce the drug?"

"No. That seems to be under control."

"Then those in most urgent need should take it first," said Abraham. "We need to set up a triage point outside and treat those with the greatest need first."

"Won't our members resent that?"

"It's possible, but relative to the people outside, they're fit and healthy. They just need to understand that it's about prioritising the worst cases and that their turn will come soon enough. In the meantime, we have an ongoing supply of the Neem extract, which has helped everyone to achieve better health with less risk. On that point, a lower risk might be considered a plus by some people, of course. We're all still seeing improvements in our health using that treatment, so it's not like we have nothing. I don't suppose it's possible to upgrade our lab to produce your new medicine?"

"Sadly not," said Leeman, "It's too complicated. A totally different method... and there might be some supply problems here too - they have greater access to the pharmaceuticals we need in Wales. We could bring some ingredients back, but that might leave the Welsh commune short, which seems rotten as they're already sharing everything they've got with us."

"OK. Scrub that idea," said Abraham.

"We just need to be patient," Leeman continued. "The team in Wales are very dedicated. They're already working on the next batch. If we want to go into production here in the Chilterns, the best approach is to see if the government boffins are ready to engage again. But I wouldn't hold my breath. I suggest for now, I administer the drug to those most in need, and then I'll head back to Wales."

Abraham nodded. "Agreed. I'll let the people here know what we're doing and why.

"Thanks. I appreciate that. I hope they understand."

"I'm sure they will. They're a good bunch."

Leeman wasn't so sure, but hoped he was right.

There was some risk involved in supplying the drug outside, as it could increase demand, cause anger and discontent among those not chosen, and create conflict and resentment, both inside and outside the commune. But Abraham felt it was the right thing to do.

With some reservations, Leeman walked through the encampments, asking who were the most diseased among their numbers. Some were brought out on stretchers, barely alive, for him to see. As he looked at how bad they were, he wondered whether they'd survive the treatment, but with their loved ones' agreement, it had to be worth a try. Otherwise they would surely die anyway.

One at a time, the diseased were brought into the compound for treatment. Taking the drugs out to them was too risky - he might get mugged. A meeting room was turned into a dormitory for the treatment of the most sick people, using old mattresses salvaged from an abandoned retail store on the edge of town.

"How come you have space? You said there was no room!" came the cry of a woman who resented being left outside.

"It's temporary - we don't have permanent space, but this is emergency accommodation for the purpose of emergency treatment."

She grumbled. Not satisfied, and others grumbled too. It was impossible to please everyone.

Inside, Leeman began the treatments, then left Melluish in charge of administering the follow up doses as he returned to Wales to help with production of the next batch.

As Melluish watched the patients' progress, the results were mixed. A couple of patients suffered from liver failure and died - their bodies unable to process the devastating onslaught of toxins from the drugs and the dying fungi. It made Melluish question the wisdom of the prescribed dose. *Would a smaller dose have been better tolerated? Would they still be alive?*

"You killed my brother!" raged a young man. Their families were furious. "Murderers! Monsters! If there was any kind of justice in this world, you'd be given the electric chair!"

It wasn't going well. But over the coming weeks, the rest of the patients improved, leaving mixed feelings and confusion in the community outside. The people who had benefited wanted to continue treatment, but it was clearly going to take some time for them to regain full health.

Two weeks later, Leeman returned with more medicine, a larger quantity this time. He and Melluish continued to prioritise patients by need, revising the doses downwards if they felt there was a risk of liver failure or complications. Some people frightened by those early fatalities didn't want to take the risk at all.

Eventually, the people outside started to disperse - either because they were feeling better, or because they had lost interest in the drug, due to its risks. It was time to treat those inside the commune who wanted to make the leap from herbal medicine, to the heavy artillery drugs that offered a more powerful solution. They didn't need persuading.

*   *   *

"David, this stuff is amazing!" Terry hugged him, then blushed. She had a soft spot for this quiet man.

"It's the formula you helped trial last year," he explained. "We finally have new supplies for all who need it... the production facilities in Wales are excellent."

He paused for thought. "I wonder how those in the bunker are getting on. I haven't heard any more from them."

"Would you expect to?"

"Well considering they threw me out and didn't want to speak to me, perhaps not. But Sgt Regan seemed keen to exchange ideas when we shared a ride to the Welsh commune a few months ago. I guess they'll come out and help other survivors when they're ready."

Jessica came by the lab after trying the new drug for a week. "I'm better! I'm cured!" she announced, delighted. "But I need some more medicine for a friend who is suffering outside. Please let me help him?"

"Is he that psycho you came in with?" Leeman asked.

"He's a good man now. Reformed," said Jessica.

"I'm afraid the answer is still No," replied Leeman. "We'll all be better off when he's dead. This isn't negotiable."

But Jessica wasn't going to let this go without a fight. Furiously, she packed her bags and left the commune, to live with Alex. "You understand me," she explained to him as they sat together on a mattress in an abandoned house - the owners presumably dead or living elsewhere. "We're the same. You feel such passion, rage and sorrow. I feel happy, then sad too."

"We do seem to 'get' each other," he said, "but Jess, didn't the commune help you? I thought you were much better there – much more contented and less emotional. Are you sure that moving out here with me is what you want to do?"

She was adamant, "I can't stop thinking about you. Spending time together really lifted my mood when we were in the clinic together. I feel a connection with you that's rare. I know you've done some bad things…"

"I've done some really bad things," he admitted.

"But you're genuinely sorry and you've changed. I can see that."

"Yes I have."

"I'm big on second chances," she continued, "and I can see past all the bad stuff to the gentle man underneath." She paused. "I love you Alex," she said quietly.

He took her in his arms and held her tight. "I love you too, Jess, but what if I give the disease back to you."

"There's a treatment now. I'll get more if I need it, and I haven't given up on you yet, either."

Chapter 43
Held at Gunpoint

Leeman headed back and forth, assisting the commune in Wales, while continuing his work in the Chilterns, always returning with more meds to help the Freedom Seekers that needed it. With hundreds living there, it was going to take time to treat everyone - some needed to continue the treatment for months. Melluish continued to produce the Neem extract on site for those who preferred to stick with the natural remedy. It was working so well for some people, that they didn't want to risk the more toxic alternative. They all kept up with their daily health regime.

*   *   *

At 10pm one dark autumn evening, while Leeman was away, a lorry crashed through the gates of the Freedom Seekers and three armed men jumped out. The man on security patrol ran to find Abraham, but they were ill-equipped for such an attack. This was a peaceful commune focused on support and healthy living. They didn't have much defence.

"What do you want?" Abraham demanded to know.

"Food and drugs!" they answered, "Give us everything you have and we'll leave you in peace. Try to con us, and we'll blast you into eternity." They shoved large guns in his face. He had no intention of arguing.

"Take everything we've got," he said, and fetched the keys to the medicine cabinet. He emptied the contents into a bag, and handed it over. "The food's in the kitchens."

"Take us there." They forced him to empty the cupboards into bags and hand it all over.

"Now leave us in peace!" Abraham pleaded. True to their word, the men left with their booty and the Freedom Seekers worked late into the night to try to reinstate some kind of fence from the wreckage.

Melluish was angry to rise in the morning and find his medicine had been stolen and they had very little food. "Why did no one wake me?" he demanded.

"They had me at gunpoint" Abraham said. "You couldn't have done anything. I just wanted to get rid of them as fast as possible, without anyone getting hurt."

"Bastards," said Melluish. "Do we know who they were?"

"No. It's a vile world out there. Could be anyone."

Melluish took a group of people off site to collect Neem leaves. "When we get back, I'll crack on producing more medicinal extract for those who need it," he said.

Upon returning with large bags full of the herb, he asked Abraham, "What are we doing about replenishing food supplies?"

"We have crops in the vegetable garden, and some from last year in store," he replied, "but it's getting critical. We did have connections with local farms, until the farmers got ill. I'll try to reconnect. Maybe the Welsh can help out with supplies until the next harvest."

"They're a small community, but I'll ask David to find out when he returns."

Terry was really upset. "We're totally defenceless," she mourned the loss of her sense of safety, security, and protection in the commune. Stephen tried to comfort her, "At least they didn't touch the vegetable plots. We can go and see if anything's ready to eat there. We should probably scour the supermarkets and warehouses again, to see if there's anything left we can take. Try not to worry. We're all together on this."

"But it's getting more difficult to stick to the health regime, with scarce supplies of some foods."

"I know, but we're getting by and we're still healthy."

There was worry in her eyes. "I don't look forward to the winter," she admitted. "It's OK in the autumn when we get a good harvest from the vegetable plots, but once the cold weather sets in, it's hard."

"We always get by though. Have faith," Stephen smiled.

She didn't look convinced, and slumped at a table with her chin resting on her hands. Abraham came by and saw Terry's obvious concern. "Chin up! It's not the end of the world," he said. "We have plenty of winter crops and some items in store. We'll be all right."

"You forget how resourceful we can be," added Stephen encouragingly.

"Remember how we were at the start?" Abraham prompted. "We're all so much better now than we were when we came in, and with this new medicine coming in thick and fast, we'll all be back on our feet again soon. We're more able to cultivate our own food in larger volumes, because we're stronger and many of us are no longer fighting disease. The future's really positive!"

Terry wasn't sure. "With all the infrastructure down and no trade, I'm not sure it's going to be easy."

"I didn't say it would be easy, but the future is bright!" said Abraham.

"Try to think positive!" Stephen said. "Lots of people have lived self-sufficient lifestyles in the past, and more people will do it in the future. Perhaps this whole disaster was mother nature telling us all to get back to our roots, stop destroying the planet, and start living simpler lives. We might be happier living this way in the long run."

"I suppose," said Terry, forcing a strained and weary smile.

*   *   *

Leeman returned from Wales with another batch of his potent cure, handing it out to those most in need. "I've brought some sacks of rice back too - they've got a glut of it!" he grinned. Terry was relieved to see him return with food!

Mark and Kevin were hanging around to see what he'd got this time. "Ooh that's good man. We need more food. Getting a bit low, especially after the raid."

He'd heard about the attack and some people's worries about food shortages. "We do need to make best use of all the land at our disposal," he said. "There are fields outside, just waiting to be sowed. Now we have a fit and healthy workforce, we need to scale up food production."

"Won't the food grown outside get stolen?" queried Kevin, now feeling healthier than he had in years. Mark and Kev had decided 'getting high' wasn't all it was cracked up to be - the commune's regime suited them nicely.

"Food theft is a risk, but one worth taking, I think," said Leeman. "If we sow in abundance and it feeds other people too, it's not a wasted exercise. Within a few more months we'll have everyone here back on their feet, and we can reach out to help other survivor communities too."

"Wow. Cool!" beamed the twosome.

Leeman's predictions were slowly coming true. Two months after re-starting the new powerful treatment, Terry was completely free from any signs of disease. She was full of life and had much more energy. She was able to help others in the commune, and take more responsibilities - things she'd been too ill to help with before.

"Want to accompany me to Wales?" Leeman asked. "I can show you their set up. It's quite interesting."

"I'd love to!" said Terry, and off they went, sharing the journey, the experience, the joy of everything finally coming together. In the car, he squeezed her hand and her heart raced. They chatted about everything on the journey and when they arrived, he took her hand and showed her round the lab. So shiny, pristine, modern. In his private apartment, they embraced, and finally kissed. This had been a long time coming, and Terry was relieved. She'd dreamed about this.

"I'd like you to be my girl," he said.

"I'd like that too," she said and they held each other tight.

Back in the Chilterns, Stephen was revitalised. His skin was clear. He felt good again. This was his second chance at life, and he was over the moon and keen to contribute where he could. He joined a work party, planting vegetables in the fields outside the commune, using seed they'd saved. There was a new enthusiasm for self-sufficiency among members of this more energised workforce. One by one, the commune's occupants were freed from the shackles of disease, but this wasn't so much the end, as the beginning of a new world. Huge challenges lay ahead.

With an increasing number of the Freedom Seekers finding complete wellness, things were starting to change. People were starting to wonder if they should lead independent lives or stick together. But it all seemed very risky in the outside world. There were dangerous gangs on the streets and no real infrastructure for food. Staying together seemed like the sensible thing to do. There was a lot of support in the commune and at a time of such dramatic change in society, that was priceless.

As new crops started to grow in the fields outside, the challenge was going to be security. In a world where everyone was struggling to find enough food to survive, the most honest, hard working, best horticulturalists may not be the best survivors, if those with armaments, aggression and a total lack of conscience stole their produce. The real answer would be to get the farms back into large scale production, so there was enough food for everyone. They would also need to focus on grains, winter crops, and produce that stored well, to get them through the hard winter months.

Chapter 44
Theft

Terry was all loved up, but worried about Jessica, who had left the commune to be with Alex. "I'm not so convinced of his reformed character," she said to Leeman, as they ate lunch together.

"Me neither," he said.

"And I'm concerned about how Jessica will get by in the outside world. She was flourishing here, but she had bipolar and mental health issues before she joined us."

He took her hand. "You know she's always welcome back, if she needs us, but she's her own woman. She has to make her own decisions."

"I know. I guess I just feel a bit protective of her. She's young and impressionable."

"And easily taken advantage of by men with their own agenda."

"Exactly. He's old enough to be her dad and their relationship is weird!"

"There's nothing we can do. She's always welcome here, if she wants to come back to us."

"I know." She poked a cherry tomato with her fork, and it squirted juice everywhere. "Haha! Sorry!"

Jessica and Alex were surviving on a stash of food taken from an out of town warehouse that, although it had been looted, still had a few items kicking around on the back of shelves and rolling around the floor. There wasn't much variety - junk food mostly, devoid of nutrition, but it kept them fed for now. They collected rainwater - a lesson learnt from the Freedom Seekers. They fell deeply in love, becoming mutually dependent on one another for support.

One day, Terry met Jessica while she was coming back from a day working on the land. "Hi Jess, Good to see you. How are you getting on?"

"Oh, you know… OK. Doing many of the same things we did inside, but without the others. I'm very happy."

"And Alex?"

"He's a wonderful loving man - passionate about his causes, as you know, but he sees the error of his ways. Therapies in the hospital helped him to empathise with other people, to control his temper. It's been hard for him, but I adore him."

"Just be careful," said Terry, "He killed someone – you have to be pretty disturbed to do that. And he's a lot older than you."

"I know, but we just connect. The age gap doesn't seem to matter."

"OK. But do ask us if you need anything won't you?"

"I asked Dr Leeman for the new medicine, for Alex. He only has a superficial infection, but it's not getting better. There's a risk he'll pass it back to me, but Dr Leeman refused to treat him."

"I can understand that," nodded Terry sadly.

Alex came around the corner and Terry shuddered. He still made her skin crawl.

"Hi," he said, "Are you ladies catching up?" He saw Terry's face. "Shall I go away again?"

"No," said Jessica, "Look," she pulled him to her side and showed off his diseased arms. "There's more underneath," she flapped his shirt.

"I deserve it Jess," said Alex. "There are ways of making my point, and the murder of an innocent woman was not the answer. Perhaps this is my penance. I don't expect these people to help me."

Terry was quite taken aback by his admission. *Has he changed? This seems surreal. Not so long ago, he wanted to kill me.*

She was uncomfortable about the whole thing, "I'm sorry, I'm expected back at the commune," her heart was racing. He frightened her and his new found humanity didn't change that – it just made him even more weird. She turned to leave.

"Please?" Jessica begged.

"Not now," Terry said as she hurried back to the Freedom Seekers.

Jessica was furious, "They're being unreasonable!"

That evening Jessica laid in bed thinking about the frustrations of the day. *I wonder if I could break in and steal some,* she thought. She pondered the idea for the next few days and then decided she should do it. She knew the weak spots - where the fence was compromised. *It shouldn't be too hard to break in*.

Aware that supplies were erratic, she wanted to ensure they had a sufficient supply of the medicine before she attempted the heist. It became a waiting and watching game.

One night, following what appeared to be a delivery from Wales, she decided to do it. "I'm breaking in tonight," she said to Alex and under the cover of darkness, she vanished round the back of the commune, climbed the fence and forced her way into the lab where the medicines were kept. It wasn't that difficult. She knew the systems, and who would be about. She dodged security and snuck into the toilet block alongside the lab. Once inside, she forced the adjoining door into the lab with a crowbar, always keeping a watch for anyone who might appear outside. A security guard came by. She could barely breathe and stayed low. He shone his torch towards the lab, decided it was nothing and continued on his rounds. In great haste, she raised the crowbar again, broke into the medicine cabinet, then she pocketed as much medicine as she could, before escaping the way she had come, back over the fence to freedom and a life of shared passion with her adoring partner, Alex.

* * *

In the morning, Leeman was furious to find the locks broken and so much of his medicine stolen. This was supposed to be a supply for anyone within the commune who still needed it, and to supply worthy people outside. They only had to ask, but he wanted to control its distribution.

"I'm bloody irritated by these fucking break ins," he said to Abraham. "We've been generous and given out plenty of medicines to people in need - sometimes prioritising people outside the commune, if their need is greater than ours!"

"Some people just want everything for themselves," Abraham sighed. "Try to stay positive. There's some left, and production is full-time in Wales now, so more batches will reach us soon enough."

"You're right," Leeman sighed. "But how did someone get in and evade all our security measures? It's got all the hallmarks of an inside job!" He was really irritated.

"I know!" said Abraham, "But security has never been our strongest point. We'll look into the breach, repair any areas of fence that have been compromised, and review our security again. Try to relax, all this stress is no good for you."

"I'm trying!" said Leeman.

Then a smile crept onto his face. "It's all quite exciting really... It's only a matter of time before we're able to reach all survivors and eradicate the disease. In the Welsh commune, they've pretty much achieved full health now. So they're reaching out to other survivors in that area to assist recovery and build new communities. I wonder what the government is doing. I haven't heard a dickey bird from them!"

"God knows. Incompetent self-interested bureaucrats," said Abraham.

"Couldn't have put it better myself," agreed Leeman.

Chapter 45
Working on the Land

Leeman arranged for a group from the commune to visit a local farmer who had received some of their medication and could benefit from help making his land more productive.

"We'd like to work together again," Leeman explained. "We can provide the people you need to get the farm fully operational. We have strong healthy people willing to work, and together we can achieve more, feed people inside and outside the commune, and start to build a new future."

The farmer was keen. "That sounds ideal. You're more than welcome to help out and share the rewards. I can't do it all by myself. It'd be a shame to overcome the disease and then starve to death!" he said jovially. "I can give your people some basic skills training, but a lot of it is simple hard graft. We'll have to grow organically as I don't have access to many agricultural chemicals. The bugs get on everything, so it can be a hit and miss affair. But the food's edible and that's all that matters, right?"

Leeman and his companions nodded in agreement. "Organic is perfect. We're all about healthy living. Besides, we have bug infestations on our plots in the commune. If the bugs like it, it means it's non-toxic and nutritious, which is good for our health." He smiled. "We're having to learn organic farming methods on the job."

The farmer seemed encouraged. "I do have machinery in the shed, but not much petrol, so I think it's going to be back to farming the old fashioned way."

"That's fine. No one is expecting this to be easy."

They worked the land with forks and shovels, and became skilled organic growers. Most of the livestock had died, except for a few chickens and stray sheep. It was a tough life and progress was slow, but they persevered and saved seed from one harvest to the next.

Leeman returned to Wales regularly to support the commune and help produce the medicine, so that survivors everywhere could benefit. They had soon beaten the disease in the Chilterns and in the Welsh commune, and were starting to share the benefit with other groups.

The Freedom Seekers, once a community of really sick people just trying to survive, had been transformed into a healthy workforce, building the beginnings of a brave new world, in the aftermath of global devastation.

Small groups of survivors travelled to the commune for medicine. Even those who had rejected the new drug after those first two deaths, eventually succumbed to the allure of a cure and a new lease of life. As time passed, the fungus was slowly eradicated from the population, as people either died or got better.

The Freedom Seekers continued to live like a big family, focused on healthy living and building a new future. It was a positive, energising environment, and they all benefited from their shared work, goals and optimism.

As they started to address the devastation outside, things weren't quite so bright. The dead outnumbered the living. Across the UK, towns and cities were like ghost towns. The clearing up effort, rebuilding infrastructure, and restoring civilisation was going to take decades.

Inside the commune, in the heart of the countryside, the Freedom Seekers had been protected - they didn't see many deaths. But in the wider world, there were issues with decaying bodies and disease. They wanted to reach out to other survivors, but faced huge challenges in the outside world.

"There are graves to be dug, sanitation issues, and a new infrastructure to be developed, connecting people living in different communities," said Abraham. He felt overwhelmed by the situation. The local villagers had created a dedicated burial ground for the deceased, in a remote part of the countryside. Now the Freedom Seekers were tasked with finishing the job.

"Urgh!" said Terry. "I'm not sure I can do this," when she realised volunteers were needed to take bodies from the village to a mass grave, making the place safe for survivors to stay there safely. Some of the refugees now called the village their home.

"Don't worry. I think we have enough volunteers," said Abraham. "I know it's grim, but it's necessary, so people don't fall ill with something else."

"Yes, I understand," she said bleakly, glad she wasn't exposed to this horror in their countryside commune.

Freedom Seekers volunteers dressed in protective clothing and masks cleared bodies from the village, piling them onto a wooden cart and hauling them to the mass grave. It was a horrible task. The smell of rotting bodies made them wretch. Some of the volunteers just couldn't hold back their vomit or their tears, but it needed to be done, to make the local area safe again.

When the work had been completed, it was considered safe to live in the village, or visit, without fear of catching a secondary disease from rotting flesh. Those involved in the clean up were monitored for signs of infection and promptly treated if necessary. This wasn't over though. They'd have the same problem as soon as they went further afield. It provided an incentive for people to stay local, for now, at least.

Up on the Welsh border, members of Kate's community were starting to rebuild their lives. As they found renewed health, they too, were able to upscale their food production, supplying neighbouring communities who needed help.

Kate was upbeat and positive. "We've been able to reach out and help others," she said to Leeman. "Since you last came by, our community has attracted new members seeking healing. So we've grown in number and started to build our own infrastructure, making new connections with surviving farmers, ensuring clean water supplies are available. We now have designated burial sites for the deceased."

"We've had to deal with that issue too," he said. "Grim isn't it."

"Yes, but necessary," she said.

The communities were like families, working together and supporting one another. Everyone had been through so much; all facing death and fear together. There was a powerful sense of community.

Relationships flourished. David Leeman and Terry built a new life together. Stephen found love with a man that he'd met at the commune, and Jessica and Alex stayed together, eventually joining another small community of survivors nearby. Kevin and

Mark continued to chill, while enjoying the sense of belonging that came with being part of the Freedom Seekers community.

Radio communications were set up between the Welsh community and the Chilterns group, to enable them to learn from each other and to work together more easily.

Across the UK, there were only a few thousand survivors. Hundreds lived at the communities in the Chilterns and on the Welsh border, but there were other small groups of survivors, who were offered medicines and supplies, if they needed them.

No one knew what was happening overseas, but the lack of incoming help suggested that the situation was similar elsewhere. What made some survivors appear to be immune? They never worked it out. Blood tests showed no abnormalities. Perhaps they'd simply never contracted the disease - or fought off a mild infection quickly, without noticing. Some had very robust immune systems and a strong sense of avoidance and self-care. Those with immunity were a bit of a mystery. Perhaps it was just part of human evolution. Survival of the fittest.

The Kayl fungus, *hot caffeine*, was still present, growing in warm shady areas in the ground, but people were very wary of it now. Everyone knew it played a role in the onset of the disease and that it should be avoided. Antibiotics were only used in emergencies - there was much more reliance on healthy living and preventative health. The new world was a very different place.

Chapter 46
The New World

20 years later...

Decades passed and all remaining evidence of the disease had been destroyed. People were generally fit and healthy, living a much simpler life. The farming system was working, and a basic level of trade and economy had risen from the ashes. A new infrastructure was in place, and small farming communities used compost toilets and got water from ground wells and natural springs. People were at one with nature again and it was as if the lifestyles of the early 21st century had never existed. Lines of communication were set up between communities, and each village had its own sources of renewable energy, and oil-powered generators, although they could be unreliable at times.

People had learnt to live with the fungus on the soil, and give it the fearful respect it deserved. No longer did anyone take it as a recreational drug. They knew it could be dangerous. No longer was it used in medicines.

There was more than enough land to go around, but some groups still managed to get into arguments about prime locations.

Many people felt uncomfortable living in the abandoned properties from yesteryear, and preferred to remain in the supportive family environment of a commune. The communes grew into villages, and developed good neighbourly relations with those living nearby. Larger communities engineered their own supplies of running water and sanitation.

A kinder culture emerged. People were more friendly, considerate and supportive of one-another. Cooperative groups did what it took to survive in the challenging conditions - but not to the detriment of others.

The Freedom Seekers were getting old now. Some had survived into their 70s, 80s and beyond. They were passing the new world onto the next generation. Most of the work was on the land.

People traded in goods and services rather than currency. Some offered farming skills, others dress-making, or building skills and everyone helped each other.

Big business didn't exist. Must-have fashions didn't exist. Celebrities didn't exist – although some people put Leeman on a pedestal. Their lifestyles were reminiscent of ancient times, but with contemporary knowledge and understanding.

*   *   *

Another 50 years later...

New generations were born who knew nothing of the deadly fungus, or how society used to be, except from seeing old books and derelict buildings that had a story to tell. Self-sufficient communities worked on the land. It was a different world, more akin to the villages of medieval England than to early 21st century civilisations.

Some of the youngsters discovered that the fungus growing on the ground caused a giggly, hallucinogenic effect that could be quite exhilarating and help them chill out. It started to catch on among the young people, and before long, it was being widely used.

Many had forgotten that the fungus was partly responsible for the infectious epidemic that swept through the strange world that their parents and grandparents grew up in. Some remembered the stories, passed down through generations, about the killer fungus and the end of the civilised world... although as it turned out, the new world wasn't so bad. People were kinder. Life was simpler. But they were always told that the fungus should be treated with respect - it could still pose a threat to the survival of the human race.

When the oldest and wisest realised that the kids were using the fungus recreationally, they told the youngsters to leave it alone. "It's dangerous!" they said, but their warnings fell on deaf ears. Anyone who had survived the epidemic was now in their senior years. Most survivors had long since passed away, leaving the new world to their children and grandchildren. Old lessons were passed down as stories and hearsay, embellished by the passing of time. Much of what they said wasn't taken seriously by the cocky adolescents who wanted to do their own thing. What did the oldies know anyway? Their paranoia was probably just dementia!

The new way of life embraced natural approaches to healing, and drew upon traditional ideas about holistic health and Eastern medicine. 21st century healthcare was a thing of the distant past. Pharmaceutical drugs weren't manufactured. Any supplies that still existed in old warehouses were now so old, they'd be useless.

Tales of the selfish, unsustainable lifestyles adopted by society throughout the 20th and early 21st centuries became the stuff of folklore and legend: a world of terrible wars and global destruction, epidemics of disease, and environmental catastrophe alongside attitudes of indifference and selfish greed. It was a world where people turned a blind eye to abuse and abandonment, where people cared more about their careers and lavish lifestyles built on debt, than about their elderly, who were dumped into the care of local authorities because they were inconvenient.

The tales of these times were told with such gusto and horror, passed from generation to generation, that they took on a life of their own - the horrors of the past, making the lifestyles of the present seem idyllic. The stories were believed by many, but the old warnings were increasingly being taken with a pinch of salt by new generations, who saw them as nothing more than mythology.

Leeman's descendents, well aware of their grandfather's role in events of the past, knew how dangerous the fungus was, but people wouldn't listen to their warnings. People used the fungus recreationally and then the local medicine-man discovered it had healing properties as a powerful antibacterial compound. It was hailed as a fantastic new breakthrough, and those who knew better, could only stand and watch in despair, as people started to use it medicinally and for recreation. Their concerns were dismissed by people who thought bacteria, not fungi, posed the greater risk to humanity. No one was listening.

Leeman's descendants had kept his antifungal formula safe, in case it was needed in the future. But when signs of the old infection started to re-emerge, they found that the fungus was mutating again and history was about to repeat itself.

The End.

If you enjoyed this book, please consider leaving a review on Amazon.